Life over Love

Life over Love

Kary Hisashima

To order additional copies of this book, contact:
Xlibris
1-888-795-4274
www.Xlibris.com
Orders@Xlibris.com
706671

PART I

Look at her. Look at how beautiful she is. No matter how long I've been with her, I never get tired of looking at her. Her name is Sandy, my Sandy. But did you know that Sandy and I almost didn't exist? Let me tell you a little story.

It was the first day of college. I decided to go to school far away from home. It was time for me to grow up and learn to be on my own. Back home, everyone knew me as Kyle. I was pretty smart, I guess, and had a lot of friends too. But for some reason, I wanted to go away. I chose this school because no one else that I knew was coming here. With the social media these days, I knew how easy it would be to stay in touch with my friends and family back home. I wanted a challenge. I knew that I would start off alone, and that was fine with me. The great unknown that lay before me was scary but very appealing at the same time.

The Roommate

I got to the campus at around 11:00 a.m. The dorm was filled with unfamiliar faces scurrying around. It made me feel at ease to know that I wasn't the only person here who was lost. I chose to live in a coed dorm. I had never lived so close to people of the opposite sex before. The floors were alternating, boys on one floor and girls on the next.

The people at the front desk were really nice. They quickly showed me around the dorm and the surrounding facilities. This one girl—her name was Laura—was really cute. I hope I would see more of her.

Finally, I got the keys to my room. My roommate was some guy named Chester. He didn't check in yet, and all that they could tell me was that he was from Chicago. I gathered my things and headed upstairs. The volunteers at the front desk helped me with my bags. I had room 205; as I approached the room, I noticed they had my name on it and Chester's too. How cool is that? I took a deep breath and opened the door. It was a nice-size room with a bed, a desk and closet on both sides, and a nice view of the courtyard.

"I'll take it," I said and thanked them for helping me with my bags.

Being left-handed, I chose the left side of the room. Don't know why, but since I had the first choice, why not? I started to unpack, placing things neatly away. *I was never this neat at home*, I thought. Maybe I am growing up.

As I was about to put my suitcase on top of the closet, I heard someone fumbling with the door. This went on for about five seconds, followed by five seconds of cursing. This must be Chester. I opened the door quickly, maybe too quickly, for I pulled Chester in with the door. It seems his key got stuck, and I guess Chester had a good grip because he went down in a heap in the middle of the room.

"Hi, I'm Kyle," I said, and I offered my hand to help him up.

"I'm Chester," he replied. "As you can see, I am a bit clumsy."

I helped Chester up, and with that, the ice was broken. Chester wasn't the biggest guy, and he had the thickest glasses I had ever seen. He didn't have many things, just a suitcase and a footlocker.

"Are you originally from Chicago?" I asked him.

"No, I am originally from Hawaii. I have only been in Chicago for a year," Chester replied.

It seems Chester's father had won the Megabucks in Vegas, and because his dad was such a huge Chicago Bears fan, he decided to buy part of the team and move there. It was kind of cool having a roommate from Hawaii. I had never been there, but I did watch *50 First Dates*. First day of college, so far, so good.

First Day of Class

I got up nice and early this morning, which is very much a rarity for me. I didn't want to be late on my first day of classes, and more importantly, I didn't want to get lost. "Chester, wake up." Chester was rolled up like an armadillo in hibernation. I couldn't tell if he was alive or dead. "Chester, you are going to be late for class."

"Go away," Chester muttered. Chester slowly got out of bed and headed for the bathroom, toothbrush in hand. It seems that we had signed up for the same English lit class, so it was pretty cool that I didn't have to walk to class alone.

"You ready, Chester?" With a nod, we were off to class. Upon finding the classroom, I was amazed at how many people were in this class with me. We quickly found seats and waited for the class to begin. I fully expected some old guy with a beard, glasses, and sweater to walk in as our instructor. Boy, was I wrong. In she came, and my jaw dropped to the desk. She introduced herself as Ms. Miller. Now I know why so many people signed up for this class, especially guys. I looked at Chester, who was too busy trying to find a pencil to notice Ms. Miller. Ms Miller had it all, nice curves, nice legs, nice upper body development, nice everything. I looked at Chester again; this time, he was trying to pick up the pencil that he had dropped on the floor. I wondered to myself if Ms. Miller did any private tutoring. Just then, I heard her say, "My door is always open should you need any extra help in my class." It is like God answered my prayer. I don't care how hard the work is. I love this class.

My next two classes were American studies and physics. They didn't quite have the scenery of English lit, and I knew that I would be very busy this semester. After my last class, I decided to check out the campus center. I walked around and found a bank, places to eat, a bookstore, and an arcade. I noticed a sign on the arcade—Help Wanted. *I could use some extra cash*, I thought and decided to inquire about the job. The manager's name was Marcus. He told me to fill out an application, and he would get back to me. The position was about ten to fifteen hours a week and started at minimum wage. I thought it would be kind of cool to work in this environment—lots of people, lot of girls—and make new friends. *First day of class, not bad*, I thought, and with that, I headed back to my dorm.

The Dorm

As I stated earlier, I chose to stay in a coed dorm. I figured it would be much easier to meet women, especially if we were all under the same roof. That night, we had a dorm social, sort of a "get to know you" party. I was very excited to be able to meet new people and make new friends. The social was to take place in the lounge downstairs.

"It's almost seven," I told Chester. "Are you ready to go?"

I could tell that Chester wasn't keen on events like this, and he didn't reply to my question.

"Chester!" I yelled. "Let's go!"

This startled Chester, I could tell.

"Yes, sir," Chester replied. "You don't have to yell."

I liked Chester. I could tell that he had a feisty streak about him, and I thought that was pretty cool.

When we got downstairs, there were already a lot of people. We were greeted at the front by one of the resident advisors.

"Here," the RA said. "Write your name on this tag and stick it to your shirt. This way, everyone will know who you are."

Chester and I filled out our name tags, and we were on the prowl. Well, maybe I was on the prowl as Chester followed me meekly around.

"Let's get some punch," I said, motioning to the refreshment table.

As we made our way to the table, something caught my eye. Or more like someone. Standing off to the side of the table was a girl talking with some other girls. She had long black hair and big brown eyes. She looked like a princess, only way prettier. Her smile was like a morning rainbow at sunrise.

I stopped in my tracks, but Chester didn't, and he pushed me smack into her, knocking her drink over in the process and all over her blouse. I quickly glanced at her name tag; her name was Sandra.

"I am so sorry for doing that," I exclaimed, although in reality, I wasn't sure if I really was.

"It's okay," she replied with a smile that almost knocked me over.

"I'm Kyle," I said meekly.

"Nice to meet you, Kyle. I'm Sandra. But everyone calls me Sandy."

She looked into my eyes, and all I could do was turn away. I didn't want her to see that I had fallen for her in three minutes.

"I better rinse this off. I'll see you around," she said, and with that, she was gone.

I turned around, and Chester had a sarcastic smirk on his face. "What a babooze," Chester said to me, laughing.

I wasn't quite sure what a babooze was, but Chester was right. I dropped the ball on that one. We headed back to our room. As I lay in bed, all I could see was Sandra smiling at me. Now I had something to look forward to tomorrow.

Tomorrow

Do you ever have those nights when you keep waking up to see if it is time to get up? So there I was at 5:45 a.m. wide awake. Class would start at 9:00 a.m. I looked over at Chester, who to my surprise was staring right back at me.

"You know," Chester said, grinning. "You owe me."

"What for?" I replied.

"Well, if it wasn't for me, you wouldn't have made a fool out of yourself and spilled your drink all over her," Chester said, trying to hold back his laughter.

Chester had a point, I must admit.

"Do you know what a lasting impression you made by ruining her white blouse?" Chester said, laughing.

I lay down and quickly fell asleep.

"Beep, beep, beep!"

I jumped out of bed and looked at the clock. It was 8:00 a.m. Chester was already dressed and doing some reading. For some reason, I wanted to look good today. I jumped up and headed to the bathroom. I could only think of seeing Sandy again.

Chester and I headed out to the cafeteria to get a quick bite. I kept an eye out for Sandy as I got my cereal and milk. To my dismay, she wasn't there. *Maybe she has an early class*, I thought. Chester and I headed to class when my phone started ringing. I didn't recognize the number, and I wondered who it was. I answered, and to my surprise, it was Marcus from the campus arcade.

"What's up?" Marcus said. "Are you interested in that job?"

"Ummm, sure," I replied. "Are you serious?"

Marcus told me to come by the arcade after class to fill out some papers and that I could probably start next week once I got used to my classes and schedule.

"I finish at two," I told Marcus. "I'll stop by then."

I looked at Chester and said, "I got a job at the arcade."

"Really?" Chester said. "Do you think maybe you could put in a good word for me?"

"I'll see what I can do," I said. I really wanted to help Chester. It would be cool if both of us could work there.

As we headed into the lecture hall for Ms. Miller's class, there she was. Sandy was actually in my English lit class. I stared at her with a look that would probably get me arrested for stalking. I didn't notice the Chester had kneeled down to tie his shoelace, and I proceeded to go tumbling over him and down to the ground in a crumpled heap, landing at Ms. Miller's feet. The entire class started to laugh, and some of the guys even started to whistle. I got up red-faced and apologized to Ms. Miller, who for some reason had a seductive smile on her face. I looked over to where Sandy was and saw her and her friends giggling with their hands over their mouths.

I thought, *God, if you have a conscience, please take me now.* This day was not what I had expected at all.

The Job

Somehow I managed to get through the rest of my classes unscathed. It was time for me to meet with Marcus at the campus arcade. Marcus was a senior, who was finishing up his degree in marketing. Since he took over as manager, the arcade has had an increased profit of 43 percent. Marcus believed that the key to a successful business was in the hands of the employees who work there. I shook hands with Marcus, and we went into his office. His office was filled with pictures of successful marketing campaigns, some old and some new.

"I looked over your application, Kyle," Marcus said. "I liked the fact that you worked for your family back home. Family businesses are the cornerstone of our society."

It was true; for four years, I worked in my family's hardware store back home. I remembered those countless days when I wished that I didn't have to work there. But looking back, I now see that it was a blessing in disguise.

I remembered what my father used to tell me, "Son, your true character is revealed by the things you do when no one is watching you."

At first, I used to hate it when he said that to me. Now it was finally starting to make sense.

"Kyle, how many hours are you willing to work per week?" Marcus asked.

I hadn't really given it much thought.

"I dunno," I replied. "I'm still trying to get used to college life."

Marcus looked at me, and from the look on his face, I knew that he understood.

"I will start you off at ten hours a week. You can add more hours later if you feel you can handle it," Marcus said confidently.

Marcus had a way of talking that made me feel comfortable.

"Sure," I said. "When can I start?"

Marcus said that I could start next week. We will go over my classes and create a work schedule at that time.

As I was walking out, I turned back to Marcus. "Do you need any more help?" I asked him.

"I'm always looking for good people who can make me look good," Marcus replied. "If you have any friends, have them come and fill out an application."

I bolted out of the arcade excited to tell Chester to sign up. I turned around to wave to Marcus when—thud!—I collided with an unsuspecting student, knocking her to the ground.

"Are you okay?" I asked embarrassingly. "I am so sorry," offering my hand to help the person up. When I saw who it was, my jaw nearly dropped to the ground. It was Ms. Miller. When she saw who I was, she gave me that seductive look again and took my hand.

"You know, Kyle," Ms. Miller said with that seductive smile, "if you keep running into me, I'm going to think that maybe you have a crush on me. And just for the record, you are kinda cute."

Ms. Miller brushed herself off and walked away. I stood there for a while, thinking if what just happened really did happen. The hottest teacher on campus thinks I'm cute? I can't wait till I go tell Chester. I headed back to the dorm, but this time, I took my time.

Where's Chester?

When I got back to my dorm room, Chester to my surprise was not there. This was strange; his last class finished at 2:00 p.m., and it was already three thirty. I tried to call his cell, but no response. *Maybe he went to the library*, I thought. I lay down on my bed and decided to take a quick nap before dinner.

I woke up to the familiar sounds of keys fumbling and a voice cursing.

"It's unlocked!" I yelled.

Chester opened the door and fell directly onto his bed, burying his face in his pillow. I could tell that something was definitely wrong.

"Is everything okay?" I asked Chester.

"I am not okay," Chester replied sadly. "I got a call from my family back home. My best friend passed away earlier today."

I sat there in shock. *Poor Chester*, I thought.

"Who was he?" I asked.

Chester looked at me sadly and put his head back down, burying it deeper into his pillow.

"He was a she," Chester said, trying to fight off his emotions.

Oh my god, I thought. I can't believe how I just managed to put my foot very deeply into my mouth.

"Who was she?" I asked in my most solemn tone.

"Her name was Lani," said Chester, his voice cracking.

"That's a beautiful name, Chester," I said. "Was she a classmate of yours?"

"No," Chester replied, a bit irritated. "She was way better. She was my pet mynah bird."

Chester proceeded to tell me how he had found Lani seven years ago lying on the road after getting hit by an errant golf ball back home in Hawaii. He took Lani home and nursed her back to health. But Lani's wing was broken in such a way that she would never fly again. He could never release Lani back into the world like that, so he decided to keep her. When Chester and his family moved to Chicago and Lani had to remain under quarantine, Chester would visit her every day with fresh bugs. Lani in return became extremely attached to Chester, learning to perch on his shoulder and saying "aloha" to everyone.

"She would even take earthworms from my mouth," Chester said, trying hard not to fall apart.

Poor Chester. I had to do something to cheer him up.

"Hey, Chester," I said with a smile, "why don't we go eat at the campus center tonight? My treat."

Chester looked up, wiped a tear from his eye, and said, "Shoots, brah. Let's go." *It's a good thing I'm getting a job,* I thought as we headed out the door.

Dinner Surprise

We made our way up to the campus center. It was about a ten-minute walk from the dorm, and the cool autumn air really felt good.

"What do you feel like eating?" I asked Chester.

Chester was busy trying to clean the lint from his pants pockets. Chester was not one to dress up. A pair of jeans, T-shirt, and jacket was the norm for Chester.

"Earth to Chester, earth to Chester," I said in a much louder tone.

"Pizza is good," Chester replied.

We headed to the pizza shop, and luckily, there was one open table left. It was pretty crowded for a weeknight, and I was starving. The smells coming from the kitchen made my mouth water. Chester and I decided to split a large pepperoni pizza with green peppers and onions. Just then, Chester got up from his chair and walked over to the other side of the restaurant. I figured that Chester needed to pee and didn't really give it much thought.

After a few minutes, I saw Chester heading back toward our table. There was a waitress following him.

Chester sat down and said, "Are you ready to order?"

I nodded to Chester, who in turn motioned me to turn around.

I turned, and before I could say anything, a familiar voice said, "Can I take your order?"

Oh my god, it was her, Sandy.

I turned to Chester who had a big grin on his face. I turned back to Sandy who smiled and said, "Do you know what you want?"

It was like I was in the twilight zone. I just froze. I wanted so badly to tell Sandy how much I wanted her, but I didn't have the guts to do it. Luckily, Chester came to my rescue.

"We'll have a large pepperoni pizza with green peppers and onions and a couple of Pepsis," Chester said, grinning ear to ear. "Hey, aren't you in our dorm?"

Sandy put her pencil to her cheek and said, "I thought you guys looked familiar. Let me get your order in."

With that, she was gone. As I watched her walk away, I couldn't help but think what a geek I was.

I looked at Chester who was staring at me disgustingly, shaking his head.

"I thought I was the only guy who didn't know how to deal with girls," Chester said sarcastically.

Then I finally came to my senses.

"You knew she worked here," I said pointing at Chester.

Chester just smiled. He had seen her there a couple of days earlier. *Chester is a better stalker than me*, I thought. I didn't want to let this opportunity go to waste, not since Chester went to all this trouble for me.

Good old Chester, I thought.

Just then, Sandy returned with our pizza.

"Here you go, guys," she said with a smile that melted my heart.

Oh my god, I thought, *what am I going to do?*

"Do you guys need anything else?" she asked both of us.

I looked at Chester who was one step ahead of me.

"Can he get your number someday?" Chester said, trying so hard not to crack up.

I nearly fell out of my chair. I gave Chester "the look," which made him laugh uncontrollably.

Sandy started to laugh also. I was just glad that it was dark, so no one could tell that I was blushing. I turned to look at Sandy who gave me a big smile.

"You've got a good friend there," she said to me, and she walked away.

I didn't know whether to beat the crap out of Chester or hug him. Chester was heartbroken earlier, but now that I saw how happy he was, it really made me feel good.

Next Day

I really didn't sleep much that night. I kept thinking about Sandy and how she smiled at me. Of course, Chester's snoring may have had something to do with me not being able to sleep. But if not for him, last night would've never happened.

I decided to get up early and do some reading. We were having our first exam for English lit class, and I wanted to go over some of the study materials. Before I knew it, I was sound asleep.

I awoke to the familiar sound of Chester's alarm blaring. I looked to Chester's bed, and to my surprise, he wasn't there. I got out of bed and saw a note left behind by Chester. The note said, "I decided to get up early and do some research at the library. I will see you in class. PS, you must've said Sandy's name about ten times last night. Actually, you only said it once, but it must have been a good dream."

Oh my god, I thought, *am I really that infatuated with her?* I got up and headed downstairs.

I was ready to head out the lobby door when I heard a girl's voice. "Hey, Kyle."

I turned around and couldn't believe my eyes. It was Sandy.

"Can I walk with you to class?" she said with that same big smile.

"Um, okay," I said in a tone that was somewhere between geeky and nerdy.

I didn't know if I was still dreaming or if I had died and gone to heaven. As we walked to class, there was so much that I wanted to say to her, so many questions that I wanted to ask her, but nothing came out. Where was Chester when I needed him? Then I began to wonder if Chester had set this up too? I smiled, which Sandy immediately picked up on.

"What's so funny?" she said curiously, still smiling.

"Oh, nothing," I said sheepishly.

We walked for another minute in silence, and then Sandy asked, "Are you always this talkative?"

I smiled and looked at her. She was already looking at me, and our eyes met. This time, she turned away shyly. *This was my chance*, I thought. This is where we separate the men from the boys. This is where I tell Sandy how I really felt about her. This is where I take control.

"What do you think about ObamaCare?" I said, wondering to myself who the hell I was.

Sandy looked at me and started to laugh. I looked at her, and I started to laugh also. Our eyes made contact again; this time, neither of us looked away. *It's funny how life works*, I thought.

"Do you believe in fate, Sandy?" I looked at her, and I could tell that this question caught her a bit off guard.

She looked straight ahead and then looked back into my eyes.

"Yes, I do," she said smiling.

We were almost to the class when, out of nowhere, Sandy turned to me and said, "Do you believe in true love?"

I was stunned. I began to look back at my short life. I had never thought about love before. I had never told anyone that I had loved them before. I came to the realization that I really didn't know what love was.

Then I heard another familiar voice. "Kyle, up here." It was Chester. He had saved a seat for me.

Sandy looked at me one last time and then headed to sit by her friends. I could tell that she was a little disappointed in my lack of an answer. During the exam, I couldn't concentrate. All I could think about was her last question to me, "Do you believe in true love?"

I was one of the last to finish the exam.

"You should have come to me for special tutoring," Ms. Miller said with her seductive smile.

For the first time ever, I felt like I really didn't know who I was or what I was doing. I needed help.

The Call

I spent that entire afternoon lying in bed, wondering about the meaning of life. *What is love?* I thought. I had dated many girls in the past and had a girlfriend or two, but nothing serious ever materialized. I kept hearing Sandy's voice asking me if I believed in true love.

I decided to call the one person who I thought could help me, my dad.

"Hey, son," my dad said, surprised to hear from me.

I haven't spoken to him much since I came to college, and I could tell that he was glad to hear from me now.

"How's school going?" he asked.

I told him that everything was going well in school and that I even got a job. I asked him how Mom was, and he said she's doing very well.

"Dad," I said meekly.

He could tell that something was up. My dad was a very perceptive man.

"Is there something wrong, son?" he said, concerned.

I took a deep breath and said, "Dad, how do you know when you're in love?"

My dad started to laugh and then said, "Dang, son, I thought that maybe you were dropping out of school or joining a cult. Who is she?"

I told you, my dad was perceptive. I told my dad about Sandy and how we first met. I told him about the stained blouse and the pizza restaurant. I told him about our walk to class and the question she asked me. I wanted answers, and I wanted them now. I was extremely desperate.

"Son," my dad said sternly, "when it comes to love, there are no wrong or right answers. Somehow, you will just know."

I thought about what my dad just told me. He was a man that I looked up to and respected very much.

"She must be a very special girl, son," my dad continued. "Just let it happen naturally."

My dad was right. Sandy was very special. I thought of her all the time. I was having feelings that I never had before, and it was a bit scary.

"Thanks, Dad," I said in a relieved tone. "Tell Mom hi for me, will ya?"

"Don't be a stranger, son," my dad replied.

"I won't, Dad. Talk to you soon."

The advice from my dad made me feel much better. I decided to do some reading when I heard a knock on my door. I opened the door; it was Sandy. She had a sad look on her face.

"Hey, would you like to come in?" I asked.

Sandy just nodded and walked into my room. I could tell that something was very wrong.

"Are you okay?" I asked Sandy with a smile.

Sandy looked into my eyes and smiled back sadly.

"I am really sorry for asking you that question earlier today," she said quietly. "It was totally inappropriate."

"It's okay, Sandy," I replied. "The question just caught me off guard a bit."

Sandy sat there silently. I could tell that there was something else bothering her.

What Sandy said next made my heart sink down to my toes.

"I need to go back home," Sandy said, trying to keep her composure. "My mother is sick."

Sandy told me that her mom had just had a stroke and that she needed help back home.

"I am going to be leaving tomorrow," she said sadly.

I was devastated.

"How long are you going to be gone?" I asked.

"I am not sure, Kyle. It could be days, it could be weeks, or it could be months."

Sandy got up and walked slowly back to her room.

"What time are you leaving?" I called out to her.

Sandy turned around and said, "8:00 a.m."

I closed my door and lay on my bed. I was sad but furious at the same time. All I wanted was to be alone. *Why is life so unfair?* I thought.

Goodbye

Chester returned back to the room shortly after. I immediately told Chester about Sandy and her mom and that she was leaving school to help take care of her, while Chester sat there stunned.

He then said, "Did you know that Sandy had approached me about you the day after you ruined her blouse?"

I looked at Chester; he wasn't making this easier.

"Everything from the dinner at the pizza place to your walk to class yesterday was planned between Sandy and me," he continued on.

I let out a big sigh, staring aimlessly at the ceiling above. We sat there silently for the next thirty minutes. The only noise was the ticking of Chester's wall clock. I had so many thoughts going through my mind. Would I ever see Sandy again? Why did Sandy ask me about true love? At this moment, for the very first time in my life, I was unhappy. I had a fuzzy feeling going through my entire body that felt like a heavy weight holding me down. These were feelings that I had never experienced before in my short life. I was sad, upset, and confused all at once.

I decided to skip dinner, take a shower, and go to bed early. Chester sensed that I needed time alone and left for the library. I lay in bed trying to sort through the feelings in my mind. *What is true love?* I thought.

Sandy had done something to me, and tomorrow, she would be gone.

I jumped out of bed to the familiar sound of Chester's obnoxious alarm. I looked at my clock, which read 7:30 a.m. I needed to say goodbye to Sandy. I grabbed my toothpaste and toothbrush and headed to the bathroom. I came back to the room to find Chester still asleep, curled up into a little ball.

"Chester! Get up!" I screamed.

Chester jumped out of bed, looked at me, and said, "What are you still doing here? Isn't she leaving soon?"

I sat down on my bed and said, "I want to see her off, Chester, but I'm wondering if it would be better if I didn't."

"Are you crazy?" Chester said fully awake now.

Chester was right. This may be the last time that I ever get to see Sandy. I grabbed my coat and headed downstairs. Sandy was already outside waiting for her ride. I walked beside her and stood there. We stood there for five minutes quietly, not even bothering to look at one another.

Then out of nowhere, Sandy spoke.

"Kyle," she said, her voice softly cracking, "I asked you about true love the other day because I thought that maybe you would be the one to help me find it. When you do find it, please promise me that you will never let it go."

Sandy's taxi had just arrived as she wiped a tear from her eye. I didn't really know what to do or say to her. She gave me one last look and got into the cab. She rolled down the window and gave me a sad smile.

The cab started to pull away; out of nowhere, I yelled out, "Stop!"

I ran to the taxi. Sandy was crying.

"Sandy," I said, barely holding it together. "No matter how long it takes me to find it, when I do, I will never ever let it go."

Sandy smiled at me one last time, and just like that, she was gone.

Chester to the Rescue

I went back upstairs to grab my books and head to the class. As I entered the door, Chester was there waiting for me. He came up to me and gave me a hug.

"Just don't kiss me," I told him, letting out a small smile.

I must admit, I needed that right then and there.

"She's gone, Chester," I said sadly. "I didn't even get her phone number."

"I think she wanted it that way," Chester said. "It probably would've made things a lot harder. This way, it's like a clean break."

Chester was right as usual. Trying to start something long distance with Sandy would have been very difficult. I began to think about the promise that I made to her. But how will I find true love if I don't know what true love is?

Then Chester said something to me that put everything into perspective at least for now.

"Kyle," Chester said calmly. "Sometimes when you love something, you have to let it go. If it comes back, then it was meant to be. If it doesn't, you move on."

Chester was right. I needed to move on, and I needed to do so now.

"You ready to go?" I said pointing at my watch.

"Shoots, brah," Chester said in his traditional Hawaiian accent.

I was having trouble in English lit class; we had our first semester term paper coming up, and I didn't know what to do it on. I remembered what Ms. Miller had told me about her door always being open.

"Ms. Miller?" I said shyly.

Ms. Miller looked at me and gave me her seductive smile and said, "What can I do for you, Kyle?"

"Could I meet up with you later today?" I said, starting to wonder if this was such a good idea. "I need help picking a good topic for my term paper."

Ms. Miller's eyes lit up, and she said, "Sure, come to my office around three thirty later today. I would be happy to help you anyway I can."

I walked away to my seat, wondering what I had just gotten myself into.

"What, score?" Chester said laughing.

Chester could be a punk, but to be honest, I really needed his friendship right now. I looked up at where Sandy used to sit with her friends. I still had a hard time believing that she was gone. Even her friends that she used to sit by in class looked a bit sad. I looked out the window; it was starting to rain. *Fitting*, I thought, *How much more depressing could this day get?*

Before I knew it, class was over.

"I'll take you to lunch," Chester said, trying to cheer me up. "Besides, it's my turn to treat."

We had a good lunch, Chester and I. To my surprise, Chester knew a lot about relationships and how to deal with the many problems that come with having a girlfriend. I began to wonder if Chester had been in love before.

We parted ways after lunch, Chester to his class, I to mine. I felt a lot better. *Good old Chester*, I thought. I was happy to be able to call him my friend.

Ms. Miller

It was 3:25 p.m.; I began to wonder if going in to see Ms. Miller was such a good idea. I walked down the hall toward her office; to my surprise, there was no one else around. I came to the door that read "Ms. Amanda Miller."

Before I could knock on the door, it flew open. "What took you so long?" Ms. Miller said with her seductive smile.

I stood there frozen. I began to imagine Ms. Miller chasing me down the hall with a lasso in her hand, riding a big white horse. The faster I tried to run, the slower I went. Then I felt the lasso around my body stopping me in my tracks, I was trapped and helpless, and Ms. Miller let out an evil laugh, coming closer and closer.

Then she said, "Are you going to stand there all day, Kyle?"

I walked in, and she closed the door behind me. Her office was filled with posters of famous athletes and famous actors in their most prominent roles.

"Have a seat, Kyle," she said, sitting down. "What can I help you with?"

I sat there for a moment and then said, "I am not sure what I want to do for my semester paper. Do you have any suggestions or ideas to help me out?"

Ms. Miller sat there for a while, then got up from her chair, and walked behind me. I was beginning to feel very uneasy when she said, "Do you like sports, Kyle? To me, there is nothing more beautiful than a finely tuned athlete doing what they do best. Look at LeBron James. You can see the determination and grit in his face when the game is on the line."

Wow, I thought. Ms. Miller is actually pretty cool. Not only is she hot but she likes sports too.

Then she continued, "Maybe you should do your paper on an athlete who transcends the line between sports and everyday life."

Ms. Miller had a pretty good idea.

I thought about it for a moment, and then I said something quite unexpected, "Could I write the paper on my roommate? He may not be famous, but I think that he has a very unique story to tell."

Ms. Miller walked back to her chair. I wasn't sure whether my idea intrigued her or made her think I was crazy.

Ms. Miller looked at me, and she wasn't smiling. Then she said, "I think that's a great idea, Kyle. No one has ever done that before. I want you to be the first."

I continued to talk to Ms. Miller for another twenty minutes. We talked about everything from sports to movies.

"I must admit," I said comfortably to Ms. Miller, "I was kinda worried about coming to see you."

Ms. Miller let out a laugh and said, "Why is that?"

"Well, you are kind of intimidating," I said, smiling.

Ms. Miller admitted to me that she can be a little flirty, but she would never cross the line or do anything unethical with any student.

"Besides," she said, "my class is one of the most popular classes on campus. The dean does notice stuff like that, you know."

I got up and thanked Ms. Miller for helping me with my paper.

"Come visit me anytime, Kyle. Good luck with your paper," Ms. Miller said, waving to me as I walked out her door.

Now, I thought, *all I need is Chester's permission.*

Chester's Dilemma

I didn't mention anything all afternoon to Chester about my paper. Something seemed to be bothering him, and I wanted to find the right time to ask him. Chester was very busy writing down notes and cursing for reasons I did not know. Chester frequently got up, paced the room, sat back down, and started cursing again. I couldn't take it anymore.

"Do you need help with anything?" I asked him.

Chester looked at me, cursed out of the side of his mouth, and said, "Is it that obvious?"

I nodded and said, "Is this about your classes?"

Chester got up from his chair, paced the room, and then sat on his bed. "No," he said angrily, "it's worse."

"Is it something to do with me?" I asked, wondering what was up.

"No," Chester said again. "If it were you, I'd just kick your ass."

Chester was not the biggest guy, but like I said before, he is one feisty bugger. Finally, Chester gave me the answer that I was looking for.

"There's this girl," he said meekly.

Chester told me how while trying to hook me up with Sandy, he had gotten to know one of Sandy's friends pretty well. Her name was Maria. Chester had a math class with her and would walk her back to the dorm after every class.

"That's awesome, Chester," I told him with a smile. "What's the problem?"

Chester looked at me and told me something that took me by total surprise.

"I'm engaged, Kyle, to my girlfriend back home," Chester said frantically.

I just sat there stunned. I didn't know what to say. This caught me totally off guard.

Chester began to tell me about Lei, his fiancé back home. Chester and Lei had been going out since their freshman year in high school. When Chester's family move to Chicago, Chester and Lei made a pact to wait for one another until their paths crossed again. They even traded class rings.

Finally, everything was beginning to make perfect sense. Now I knew why Chester knew so much about relationships and girlfriends.

"Kyle," Chester said worriedly, "I don't want to lead Maria on, but I'm afraid that if I tell her the truth, she won't be my friend anymore."

Chester sat back down at his desk. I knew that he was waiting for me to say something intelligent.

I sat there for a moment, and then I said to him, "Chester, you have to tell Maria the truth. Besides, how sure are you that she wants a relationship with you?"

Chester turned around and looked at me.

"You know what, Kyle," he said politely.

I fully expected him to call me a babooze again, but to my surprise, he turned to me and said, "You are absolutely right. I don't know."

Now was the time, I thought.

"Hey, Chester, can I ask you a favor?" I said.

Chester looked at me and said, "Shoots, name it."

"I would like to do my semester paper on you," I said to Chester. "I believe that you have a story to tell, and I would like to tell it."

Chester looked at me stunned. "Why would you want to write about me?"

"According to Ms. Miller," I told Chester, "writing about a roommate has never been done before, and she gave me her blessing. Let me tell your story, Chester."

Chester looked at me. He could tell how much this story meant to me.

"I would consider it an honor," Chester said proudly. "Just change the names to protect the innocent, will ya?"

Awesome, I thought, *I finally had my topic.*

Then Chester said, "But first, I have to go talk to a girl."

Chester left the room. I knew where he was going, and I hoped that everything worked out for him. I sat there for a moment, and then I began to think of Sandy. Even though I hardly knew her, it was like she took something from me when she left. All of these feelings and emotions were new to me, and I really didn't know what to do.

The Interview

I decided to make my paper into a semiautobiography. Of course, the paper would be based on Chester's life, but at the same time, I thought that it was necessary to protect Chester's identity. I already knew of Lani, his mynah bird, and Lei, his fiancé, but I was curious to learn more about my roommate and good friend.

That night after dinner, I began my interview with Chester. I wrote down a bunch of questions to ask him beforehand, and I let Chester look them over. If there were any questions that he felt uncomfortable with, he could cross them out. To my surprise, not a single question was crossed out.

"Okay, Chester, you ready?" I asked nervously.

Chester nodded, and the interview had officially begun. I turned on my tape recorder. "Chester, tell me more about your childhood."

In all, my interview consisted of ten questions. Chester did a great job of answering each and every question for me. In less than two hours, the interview was over. To thank Chester, I decided to take him for a late-night snack.

We headed to the campus center to get some ice cream. Being a weeknight, there were not a whole lot of people up there. There was the normal crowd of students who didn't study and their counterpart, the students who were so smart that they didn't have to study. I decided to check out Marcus at the arcade. We walked into the arcade; there were a few students shooting pool and some others playing video games. Marcus was sitting at his desk reading a book on marketing concepts. *Typical Marcus*, I thought.

"Hey, Marcus," I said, shaking his hand. "How's it going tonight?"

"Hey, Kyle," Marcus said with a smile. "You ready to work some nights? I could use a night or two off a week."

Marcus was very particular who worked for him, and he always worked nights, so it was a very big honor for him to ask me to work nights.

"I'll think about it," I said, trying not to show how excited I was. "By the way, Marcus, this is Chester, my roommate."

Chester and Marcus shook hands. Unfortunately, Chester's hand had some ice cream on it.

"Good firm sticky grip you got, Chester," Marcus said sarcastically, grabbing a wipe to clean his hand.

"Are you looking for anymore help, Marcus?" I said trying to hide Chester who was now licking the ice cream from his hands.

Marcus handed Chester an application and told him to fill it out and bring it back tomorrow.

Then Marcus said, "Why don't you stop by also, Kyle? We can talk about you filling in for me a couple of nights a week."

I thanked Marcus and so did Chester. I could tell that Chester was excited about possibly working for Marcus.

As we headed back to the dorm, Chester caught me by surprise. "I am lucky to have you as a friend," he said to me with a smile.

No, Chester, I thought, *I am the lucky one.*

The Paper

After three weeks of hard work and lots of ice cream, my paper was finally over. Of course, I could not turn it in without Chester's approval, and after editing a paragraph or two, the paper finally was complete. I must admit, I thought it was really good. I just hope that Ms. Miller feels the same way.

I decided to go to class early. I wanted to give Ms. Miller a thank-you gift for helping me with my paper. I decided to go to Ms. Miller's office.

Ms. Miller was just about to lock her office door when I called out to her. "Hey, Ms. Miller, wait up."

"Hey, Kyle," Ms. Miller said with her usual seductive smile.

"I have a gift for you, Ms. Miller." I opened my backpack and took out the gift. "I just wanted to thank you for helping me with my semester paper."

I handed Ms. Miller the gift. I could tell that this caught Ms. Miller off guard. In fact, she looked a bit flustered. She opened the gift. It was a poster of LeBron James dunking an alley-oop pass from Dwayne Wade.

"This is awesome, Kyle," Ms. Miller said. "I am going to put it right here beside my desk."

"I'll see you in class, Ms. Miller," I said, walking away.

"Wait, Kyle, I have something I want to give you." She motioned me to come toward her, which I did. "Now close your eyes, Kyle."

I closed my eyes, wondering if she was going to tie me up or something. Instead, I felt her take my hand and open it. Then she placed something in it and closed it. I opened my eyes and opened my hand. It was a little keychain with a four-leaf clover in it. I looked at Ms. Miller, and for the first time, Ms. Miller was smiling at me without the seduction.

"Watching you this whole semester, I felt like there was something bothering you."

I sat there, listening to her in awe. How did she know?

"Anyway," she continued. "We all need a little luck now and then to help us get through hard times. When I saw this keychain, I immediately thought of you."

I didn't know what to say or do. Now I was visibly flustered. Then I did something totally unexpected. I walked up to Ms. Miller and gave her a hug. I wasn't sure what Ms. Miller was thinking, but boy, did she feel good. Then she hugged me back, and that's when I noticed, boy, she smells good too.

"We better go to class now. Kyle," Ms. Miller said, straightening her blouse and flashing that seductive smile. "People may start to get suspicious."

I walked out of her office and headed to the classroom, where Chester already was. I took the keychain she gave me and quickly attached all of my keys to it. Ms. Miller was right. I needed a little bit of luck.

I began to think of Sandy. I wondered what she was doing right this minute. I wondered if her mother was okay. I wondered if I would ever see her again.

Time Flies

Do you ever wonder where the time goes? My first semester of college was nearly over. Although I did really well in school, had a blast at my job, and found a new best friend, there was something empty about my first semester of college. I wondered if Sandy would be coming back to school. I wondered if her mom was better. I told myself that I shouldn't worry about things that I cannot control, but to no avail. I grabbed a few more things and stuffed them into my suitcase. I was actually looking forward to going back home, I missed my family, and maybe they could help me take my mind off Sandy. Just then, Chester barged into the room, breathing heavily. He looked as though he had seen a ghost.

"What's up?" I asked Chester curiously.

Chester took off his parka, shook the snow out of his hair, and said, "Oh my god! Guess what?"

"I give up," I told Chester anxiously.

"Lei is coming to Chicago to visit me."

I was happy for Chester, and I could tell that this was really a big deal for him. In a way, I was jealous of Chester. He had found his true love and had managed to keep it alive despite being so far away from Lei. At the same time, I was saddened by the fact that I wouldn't see him for almost a month.

"She's coming to Chicago, Kyle. She's coming to see me," Chester was nearly shouting by now, and his attempt at a moonwalk left much to be desired.

"Hey, Chester, why don't we go celebrate? My treat."

Both of us were leaving the next day. Chester has been like a crutch for me through this whole semester. Whenever I needed someone to lean on, Chester held me up. Having a friend like that took a lot of pressure out of life. Although I had many friends back home and I was very much looking forward to seeing them, none of them could compare to Chester.

We ate pizza that night in the very same restaurant where Sandy worked. Although this was supposed to be a joyous evening, it was anything but that for me.

I woke up the next morning to the familiar sound of Chester's blaring alarm. My cab was coming at 10:00 a.m. to take me to the airport. I headed downstairs into the lobby to check my mail. As I was heading back upstairs, I ran into Maria, Sandy's roommate. We smiled at one another as we passed by. Then she called my name. I turned to Maria who had a smile on her face.

"I have a message for you, Kyle, a message from Sandy."

My eyes lit up. "What is it?"

"Sandy wanted me to tell you that she will be back next semester. Her mother has made a full recovery and is doing very well."

I was so happy that I gave Maria a great big hug. At first, Maria didn't know how to react, but when she saw how elated I was, she hugged me back as well.

"Thanks, Maria," I said like a little boy at Christmas.

I thought, *Christmas is coming early for me.* I ran back to the room to break the news to Chester. It's so funny how life keeps throwing us these curves. Just last night, I was depressed about life. Today life was grand.

Coming Home

"Kyle. Hey, Kyle, are you really here?" a familiar voice called out.

I felt my bed shake. About then, I realized that I was finally home. "Hey, Kyle, I wanna play with you."

I got in late last night, and my baby brother, Kevin, was already asleep. It felt really good to be home again. I missed my family and my friends, and I even missed my pesky little brother. I got out of bed and went into the bathroom to get washed up before breakfast. I headed downstairs to the familiar smell of Mom's awesome biscuits.

"It's about time you got up," my mom said with a smile. "Your father wants you to come by the hardware store later to help him out."

"Aw," Kevin said in his usual whiny tone, "does this mean that Kyle can't play with me?"

"Did you clean your room young man?" Mom said, pointing a spatula at Kevin.

"No," Kevin said pouting.

"Clean your room because Grandpa and Grandma will be over for dinner, and you know how Grandpa likes to take a nap in your room."

Kevin went upstairs to go clean his room while I took a bite of one of Mom's awesome biscuits. It was nice to catch up with Mom again, and we spent an hour shooting the breeze.

After breakfast, I decided to go to the hardware store early. Dad needed my help putting together some new displays, and I liked doing stuff like that. I entered the hardware store to the familiar smiles of Rob and Wanda. Rob and Wanda had been working in the hardware store since I was five. In a way, they helped raise me, having to put up with my endless hours of running around the store. I found my dad already trying to put up a new display for a lawn mower.

"Hey, Pops," I said, patting him on the back.

"Hey, son," he replied. "Give me a hand."

We worked on that display for about an hour with hardly a word said. Then out of nowhere, my father asked, "So how's your love life going, Kyle?"

I nearly swallowed my gum when I heard that question. I told my dad about Sandy and what happened to her mom. I also told him what Sandy said to me about true love and how she had to leave school to care for her mom.

"Sounds like quite a girl, son," my dad said with a smile.

I went on to tell him how Sandy was always on my mind and that she was coming back to school the upcoming semester. My dad sat there silently for a moment, staring at the lawn mower display. Then he told me something that put everything into perspective.

"Son," he said in his stern tone, "some people spend all of their lives looking for love and not finding it. That being said, sometimes love finds you. Regardless of how it happens, you need to put the work into it. Being in a relationship is a full-time job and has the potential to be a lifelong commitment. Take it slow. Your mother and I dated for six months before we even held hands. Remember, in love, there is no right or wrong answers. Kyle, somehow you will know."

We managed to finish that display in about an hour. "I'm going to go home and play with Kevin," I told my dad.

My dad smiled and told me to have fun. As I left the store, I began to think about what my dad had said. I couldn't wait to go back to school and see Sandy. I really did miss her.

Mom and Me

I went home early to play with Kevin, but to my surprise, Kevin was over at his friend's house to play video games. Mom was home; she was making one of my favorite meals, beef stew.

I missed Mom's cooking while away in college, and of course, she noticed. "Have you lost weight, Kyle? Usually, you gain weight when you go away for college."

Mom was right, my pants got looser as the semester went by. Hopefully, a couple of weeks of Mom's cooking will make my pants fit perfectly again.

Mom made us a couple of cups of hot chocolate and told me to have a seat with her at the dinner table.

"So who is this girl who has my son tied up in knots?" my mom asked smiling.

"What did Dad tell you?" I asked my mom, laughing.

"Oh, just something about you asking about love. You know, Kyle, I'm the one you should be asking about love."

"C'mon, Mom," I said sarcastically. "You know that when it comes to stuff like this, I need help from the male perspective."

"Pardon me," my mom said, turning her face away with her eyes closed and nose up in the air.

I told my mom about Sandy and how we met and how she had to go home to care for her ill mother before anything could happen. I told her what she said to me about finding true love and never letting it go and how she would be coming back next semester.

"Do you think that she is the one?" Mom asked me in a more serious tone.

"I don't know, Mom. I never really got the chance to find out."

Mom sat there quietly for a moment. Then she told me something that I didn't expect to hear from her.

"Kyle," she said solemnly. "Your dad has been under a lot of stress lately. When that super hardware store opened downtown, it really cut into his business. His blood pressure has been very high lately, and he continues to work long hours, trying to compete. I am very worried about him."

Now it was my turn to sit there quietly. He never told me, but that was Dad. He was a very proud man who built up our business from scratch. Everyone in our town knew Dad's store, but like anything else, a good thing doesn't always last forever.

My mom sat there quietly. I knew there was something else on her mind.

"What is it, Mom?" I asked her.

Mom sat there staring at the window. Then without looking at me, she said, "I was hoping that maybe you could stay home this semester and help your dad out. I'm afraid that if he tries to keep up this pace, his health may get worse. You could still go to school, but maybe you could enroll at the local junior college for now. I am very worried about your father, Kyle. If anything were to happen to him, I don't know what I would do."

I could see the fear in my mother's eyes, and I could hear the fear in her voice. I began to think of my dad and all the sacrifices that he made for our family. Then I thought about Sandy.

"Anyway, Kyle," my mother interjected, "please consider it. That is all that I ask."

I was at a crossroads here. Do I stay home and help my dad? Or do I go back to school and find out if Sandy was the one? I went upstairs to go lie in my room. I just wanted to be alone.

The Dream

I must have dozed off, but while I was sleeping, I had a dream. In my dream, I was back at college. I was in my room studying when Sandy came into my room and gave me a hug, "Don't worry, Kyle, I will wait for you," she said smiling with tears running down her face.

"How did you know?" I said to her.

She put her finger on my lip, "Because I found true love, Kyle, and I will never let it go."

I woke up more confused than I was before I fell asleep. I went back downstairs to eat dinner. Mom's stew smelled delicious. Dad didn't come home yet, and Mom and Kevin were at the table eating dinner.

"Did you have a nice nap?" my mom asked.

"He must have been dreaming about the beach," Kevin said with a mouthful of stew. "He kept saying 'sandy.'"

My mom smiled and told Kevin not to talk with his mouth full. About then, Dad came home. He came into the house and gave my mom a kiss. He looked very tired and a bit pale.

"How was your day?" Mom asked.

"A little slow," Dad said, half smiling. He then turned to me and said, "Hey, Kyle, can you give me a hand moving some things around the store tomorrow?"

"Sure thing," I said. "No problem."

We all sat around the dinner table just like the good old days, talking about the day and what each of us did. Then Dad excused himself from the table and went upstairs. I could tell that he was beat.

The next morning, I woke up early. Kevin was already up, playing video games and screaming at the television.

"Hey, Kyle, come and play with me," Kevin blurted.

I sat down on the couch and challenged him to Mario Kart. There was once a time when I used to beat Kevin with ease, but the little bugger has been practicing, I could tell.

"Hey, Kyle, can I go to the store with you?"

"Sure," I replied. "Just don't drive everybody nuts."

I continued to play with Kevin, and I began to wonder if he had any idea of what was going on with the store and Dad's health. Kevin was only ten years old and had so much life ahead of him. How would he take it if anything happened to Dad? Mom popped her head into the living room and told us that breakfast was ready.

"Come on, Kev, we better eat and head to the store."

Kevin put down his controller and ran into the kitchen. Seeing Kevin so happy and excited made me remember how it was when I was his age. I used to be so excited when Dad let me stay with him at the store. I remembered all the times Dad took off from work to take me to baseball practice, how he played catch with me during the long summer afternoons, or when he made me that soap box derby cart that I used to ride up and down the street as a kid. And that's when it hit me. Suddenly, everything became very clear, and I knew what I had to do.

At the Store

When we got to the store, Dad and Rob were busy putting away some new inventory that had just come in. Kevin ran to Wanda and gave her a big hug. Of course, Wanda reached into her pocket and pulled out a piece of bubble gum. It didn't take much to make Kevin happy.

Dad and Rob were just finishing up when some customers came in. Rob went to help the customers, and Dad went into his office. *This was my chance*, I thought. I knocked on the door and walked in. Dad was looking at some invoices, scratching his head. Dad did things old school with lots of paper and lots of file cabinets.

"Hey, Dad, you got a minute?" I asked.

"Sure, son, what's up?"

I sat down and pulled out a piece of paper from my pocket. "Dad, I have decided to stay home and help you with the store."

Dad looked stunned. He sat there for a moment, staring at his desk.

"Son," he said, "what about school?"

"I can take some classes at the community college here in town. Dad, Mom told me everything. I know that you haven't been feeling well lately, and she is very worried about you and your health."

Dad got up and walked to the window overlooking the store. "Son, I can't keep you from pursuing your dream, and what about that girl?"

Why did he have to mention Sandy? Low blow, Dad.

"Dad, this store is our life. Right now, this is where I need to be. I wrote down some ideas about how we can better market the store. I want to computerize everything, increase advertising, and go head to head with that big box store."

Dad looked at me. I could tell that his eyes were tearing up. "You really think that we can turn this thing around, Kyle?"

My head kept telling me, "What are you getting into?" But the words out of my mouth said something totally different.

"Dad, I know we can do this. I have a friend that I met in school. His name is Marcus. He is a marketing genius, and I think that he can really help us. He believes that businesses like ours are the cornerstone of our society and what America was built on."

Dad had a proud look on his face.

"I believe in you, son," he said with a smile. "You do what you need to do, and I will support you 100 percent."

Just then, Kevin popped his head into the office. "Does this mean that you are staying home, Kyle?" he said bright-eyed and bushy-tailed.

I looked at Dad who nodded his approval.

"You bet, Kevin," I said proudly.

"Oh boy," Kevin yelled at the top of his lungs.

Kevin went dancing off through the aisles of the store while Dad and I walked around, exchanging ideas on what we could do to make the store better. I hope that I didn't bite off more than I can chew. Even though this meant that I would not be seeing Sandy, I knew that at this stage in my life, this was the right thing for me to do. For the first time in my life, I was going to try and make a difference, and it felt really good. I just hope that Sandy understands.

PART II

Look at him. That's my Kyle. He may be goofy, he may be silly at times, but he is the one, the man who I decided to spend the rest of my life with. Did you know that Kyle and I almost didn't exist? Let me tell you a little story.

The Wait Is Over

I spent all night tossing and turning. Never before had I been so nervous about the next day. I must have looked at my clock a hundred times last night, and you know the saying about a watched clock and how it never moves.

"Sandy, did you even sleep at all last night?" It was the familiar voice of my mother.

Since her stroke, my mother had recovered remarkably well. "Not really," I replied groggily. Even she could tell that I hardly slept.

"Come to the kitchen. I have a pot of coffee brewing, extra caffeinated."

As you can probably tell, Mom and I were very close. Father died when I was three years old, and she had to raise my sister and I single-handedly. Even through the toughest times, we managed to pull through. My sister got a job after high school and was actually doing quite well managing a small cleaning company. Before her stroke, Mom used to manage the cafeteria at our local high school. Now she has limited use of her left arm, and she may not be able to go back. I owe everything to her, so coming home to care for her was a real no-brainer. I entered the kitchen; Mom was cutting fruit. Since her stroke, she had really watched her diet and looked fabulous.

"You know, Mom, the boys are going to notice you more than they notice me," I said with a smile.

My mom just smiled. I could tell that she was blushing. I joined her at the kitchen table, and she brought me a cup of coffee.

"You know, Sandy, I can't thank you enough for all that you've done for me these past four months. I am sad to see you go, but it's your time now."

I could see Mom's eyes start to tear up. "I'm your mother. I know you better than you know yourself. What kept you awake last night?"

I did not tell Mom about Kyle. I guess I never really had the chance. But now that she was better, maybe it was time for me to tell her.

"Mom, when did you know that Dad was the one?"

I could tell that this question caught my mom by surprise. But her answer was even more surprising.

"I knew from the first time I met him," she said, playing with her hair. "When your father left for military duty, we had only been dating for about a month. But when he had to leave me, that was when I knew for sure. And I think that he knew it too. You see, Sandy, some people spend their entire life looking for love. Sometimes you just know. Your father and I knew right away as soon as he came back home to me. Why do you ask?"

I took a sip of coffee and smiled at my mother.

"I think something like that has happened to me," I said to her smiling.

My mother's eyes got big, and she covered her mouth with her hand. "Is he someone from school?"

"Yes," I nodded. I could see the questions coming from my mother's eyes.

"Well, don't hold back," she said excitedly. "Do tell."

I told my mom about Kyle and how we met. I told her about the punch spilling on my blouse and how his roommate had set up our meeting at the pizza parlor on campus. Looking back, I knew Kyle for such a short period. So why did I have such strong feelings for him? Why do I constantly think of him all day long?

"When did you know?" my mother asked solemnly.

Now it was her turn to catch me by surprise. I thought about it for moment, and then I looked at my mother, and this was my response, "I knew that day when I had to leave him."

Tears were running down my mother's eyes. "We need to get you back to school," she said, wiping the tears with a napkin.

Yes, this was the day that I had been waiting for. It was finally here.

Back in School

I arrived at the campus a little before 6:00 p.m. My roommate Maria was already in the room; she had gotten back much earlier during the day. As I entered the door, Maria ran to me, giving me a great big hug.

"How's your mom doing?" she said smiling.

"She's almost fully recovered, thank you so much for asking," I replied.

Maria was such a good friend, and I really missed her dearly. She was the one who set up the pizza dinner along with Chester. Then my attention turned to someone else. She could see it in my eyes.

"He's not here yet," Maria said as though she had read my mind. "Chester isn't here either."

We decided to meet some other friends and grab dinner up at the campus center. I hoped that when I returned, Kyle would be there in his room. We decided to eat pizza, and I was hopeful that I could see the manager and ask for my old job back.

We spent a couple of hours laughing and catching up. It was so good to be back with my old friends again. When we got back to the dorm, I went straight upstairs to Kyle's room. When I saw the door open to his room, my heart started to beat like a drum. What was I going to do? What was he going to do?

"Knock, knock," I said, looking down at the floor.

I heard a familiar voice say, "Come in."

I entered the room, but to my surprise, there was only one person in there. I looked around. Kyle's side was completely bare and untouched.

"I think you should have a seat, Sandy," Chester said to me in a serious tone.

I sat down on Kyle's bed, preparing for the worst. Chester could see the fear building in my eyes and quickly said, "Sandy, there is nothing wrong with Kyle. He is perfectly fine."

When I heard that, it was like a huge weight had been lifted off me.

"But," Chester continued on, "he isn't coming back to school this year."

I sat there stunned. I wasn't prepared for this, and I really didn't know what to say. Chester came over and sat next to me. "He decided to stay home, Sandy. I am going to miss him too."

Chester told me about Kyle's decision to stay home and help his dad with the family business. Chester went on to tell me about the store doing poorly and the declining health of Kyle's father.

"Kyle called me two nights ago and told me the news. It was a very hard decision for him, Sandy, and you were the reason why it was so hard. Right now, he just feels that home is where he needs to be."

I began to think why life was so unfair to me. I was sad yet upset at the same time. Then Chester told me something that brought me back to reality.

"Sandy," he said, "Kyle wanted me to give you this message." He reached into his pocket and pulled up a piece of paper. "He e-mailed this to me to give to you. I didn't even read it."

I took the letter from Chester's hand, thanked him, and headed back downstairs to my room. A feeling of numbness came over my entire body.

When I got to my room, Maria knew that something was wrong. I put the letter on my desk and lay down on my bed. For some reason, I was afraid to read the letter for fear of what it might say and also because I wasn't sure if I could take much more. Exhausted, I quickly fell asleep.

The Letter

"Sandy, get up. Sandy, if you don't get up, you are going to be late for class." As I opened my eyes, Maria was standing over me, with her hands on her hips.

"I thought you were in a coma," she said sarcastically.

I looked at my desk; the letter was still there. I stumbled out of bed and got ready for class. Before heading off to class, I grabbed the letter from my desk and put it in my pocket. Outside, Chester was waiting to walk with us to class. As we walked to class, it didn't take long for Chester to break the ice.

"What did the letter say, Sandy?" Chester asked excitedly.

I continued walking, pretending that I didn't hear him, but Chester was his usual relentless self.

"Sandy," he said loudly, "you are killing me."

"I didn't read it yet, Chester," I said to him sadly.

Chester could hear the sadness in my voice and backed off. *Poor Chester*, I thought, *He just cares.*

I had three classes today, and it was as though I really wasn't there for any of them. I couldn't take it anymore. I needed to know what was in the letter. I went to the campus center arcade, where Kyle used to work. I took the letter from my pocket. I sat there for several minutes just staring at the letter while my eyes started to tear up. I slowly opened the letter, and this was what it said:

> Dear Sandy,
>
> From the moment that I first saw you, I knew that you were the one. I could not go a single minute without thinking of you. Do you remember that day you asked me if I believe in true love? To be honest with you, I had never really given it much thought. I had no reason to up until that time. When you left school to care for your mother, it was as though a part of me left with you. That's when I first realized that true love really does exist. The feelings that I felt at the time were all so new to me. Never before had I felt the emotions that I felt being with you even for that short period. But Sandy, life is full of crossroads, and I have come to mine. If you remember, you also once told me if I ever find true love to never let it go. I have found true love, Sandy, but right now, I have to let it go. For whatever reason, we seem to be destined to be apart. Faith has not been kind to us, but maybe this is our destiny. Sandy, this is where I belong, and I cannot ask you to wait for me. You are a special person, with full of love to share. You need to go on with your life as I will go on with mine. I will never forget you, and I'm so blessed to call you my friend.
>
> Love,
> Kyle

I got up and threw the letter into the trash. As I walked back to the dorm, tears began to run down my cheeks, but deep inside, I was furious. How could life treat me like this? All my life, I tried to do the right thing. I needed answers, but who could I turn to?

Friends

I got back to my dorm room. Maria and Chester were there waiting for me. They could tell that I was very upset. I lay on my bed and buried my head in my pillow. Chester got up, said goodbye, and headed back to his room.

"Hey," Maria said, "wanna talk about it?"

I sat up and turned to Maria. "Let's go out for dinner. Tell Chester to join us."

Maria smiled and ran upstairs to go tell Chester. I knew that Maria had a thing for Chester; it was only so obvious. Watching her so excited made me think about Kyle. I wondered what he was doing right at that moment. I wondered if he was thinking about me.

I could hear Chester and Maria coming back to the room. I grabbed my things, and we headed up to the campus center. We walked past the pizza parlor where I used to work. I remembered that night when I served Kyle and Chester like it was just yesterday.

We decided to eat at the sandwich shop. We ordered and sat down. Maria's phone began to ring.

"It's my mom," she said, covering the phone with her hand. "I'm going to take this outside."

"You know, Sandy," Chester said suddenly. "I have also lost someone very close to me."

"Did someone pass away in your life, Chester?" I said sadly.

"Not quite," Chester replied. "My fiancé Lei was supposed to come to Chicago to see me. I was so happy to be able to see her, but at the last moment, she cancelled."

I could tell that Chester was really bummed. In a way, it took my mind off Kyle.

"Lei was supposed to come to Chicago to see me over the break," Chester continued on. "But two days before she was to arrive, she called me to tell me that she was not coming and that she was breaking off our engagement. I asked her why. She went on to tell me that she had met someone else. Some surfer dude from Maui named Keoki. You know, Sandy, at first, I was really upset. But now I think it may have been a blessing in disguise. Sandy, can I ask you something? What do you think about me and Maria?"

A smile came over my face. I almost forgot what a smile felt like.

"Chester, you and Maria are perfect for one another. And she's crazy about you."

Chester began to blush. Right then, Maria came back to the table and sat down.

"Chester, why are you so red?" Maria asked curiously.

Chester just sat there with a sheepish smile on his face. He then held his hand out to Maria. Maria looked at Chester's hand and then looked at Chester who was still smiling sheepishly. Then Maria took Chester's hand. Chester's eyes got big, and he pumped his fist to the sky.

"Oh yeah!" Chester yelled, making everyone in the restaurant stare at us. Maria and I just laughed.

I was so happy for them. *Chester and Maria are so good for one another*, I thought. I began to think about Kyle again, and just like that, again, I was sad.

Time Drags On

They say that time flies when you're having fun. For me, it's more like time drags on when you're all alone. I've been back at school for only a month, but it seems like a year. Chester and Maria's relationship has really taken off, and I appreciate the fact that they always invite me to do things with them. It is really hard to be the third wheel, and although I am very happy for Chester and Maria, seeing them together always seems to make me think of Kyle. For whatever reason, I can't get myself to move on from this. I've been asked out on numerous occasions, but I have turned every guy down. I am even asked out by a girl. Go figure.

Today in Ms. Miller's class, she announced that she would be meeting with all the students individually to discuss topics for the semester paper. There would be a sign-up sheet posted outside the classroom door after class.

Every day that I attend Ms. Miller's class, I always ended up staring at the seat where Kyle used to sit. This was the one class that we shared, but because I dropped out last semester, I needed to take it again. I would sit in class staring out the window and begin to wonder what Kyle was doing right now. Was he thinking of me? Did he find someone else? It was like a pattern.

After class, I looked at the sign-up sheet. I decided to sign up for the first available time, which was later today at 3:30 p.m. I finished my last class at three, so it worked out well.

As I was walking to my next class, I heard a familiar voice calling me; it was Maria.

"Hey, Sandy," she called. "Why are you walking so fast?"

I didn't quite know how to answer that. I wasn't even aware of how fast I was walking.

"This afternoon, Chester and I are going to go to the mall. Do you want to come?"

Maria was such a good friend, always thinking of me.

"It's okay," I said with a smile. "I have to meet Ms. Miller at three thirty. You guys go ahead. Have fun."

"Thanks, Sandy, we will. I'll see you at dinner." And with that, Maria headed for her next class. *They should spend more time alone anyway*, I thought.

My last class of the day was biology. I was actually looking forward to today's class. We were going to dissect real frogs. I began to daydream about my frog, which suddenly jumped up and came to life.

"Please don't cut me," the frog said to my surprise. "I am really a prince who was put under a powerful spell by the evil queen. I will remain a frog until I receive a kiss from my true love."

"Do you want me to go catch a girl frog for you to kiss?" I told the frog.

"No," said the frog angrily, "I am really a prince, and I need the kiss of another human."

Against my better judgment and because it was a dream, I decided to kiss the frog. The frog puckered his slimy green lips, and I kissed him. The frog leaped from my hands and disappeared into a cloud of smoke. Then I saw a man appear with a crown on his head. His back was toward me, but when he turned around, it was Kyle.

"I finally found true love," he said to me smiling.

I then tripped over a bush and woke up from my daydream. Embarrassingly, I picked myself off the ground and proceeded to head to the class.

My Meeting with Ms. Miller

It was time for me to go meet Ms. Miller. I headed to her office right after my last class. Her office door was open, and Ms. Miller was busy grading some papers.

"Knock, knock," I said politely.

Ms. Miller looked up at me, smiled, and said, "Come in, Sandy."

I entered her office and sat down. Ms. Miller was pretty much the coolest teacher on campus, and sitting in her office, I could see why. Her office was filled with cool posters of famous celebrities and athletes. Also, she was drop-dead gorgeous.

"I'm so glad you are back in school," Ms. Miller said smiling. "How's your mother doing?"

"She's doing great," I replied.

"And how are you doing?" Ms. Miller's question caught me off guard a bit.

"I'm doing okay, I guess," I replied, trying not to make eye contact with Ms. Miller.

"Sandy, I've been doing this too long. I know that everything is not okay with you."

Oh great, I thought, *Ms. Miller could see right through me.*

"Sandy, you were one of my better students until you had to leave school. This semester, your work is average at best. You look disinterested in class, and I can tell that something is bothering you."

"I'm sorry," I said quietly. "I have had a lot on my mind since my return."

Then Ms. Miller turned to me and said, "This is about a boy, isn't it?"

I was shocked. Ms. Miller was reading me like an open book.

"Yes, Ms. Miller," I said meekly, "it is about a boy."

Ms. Miller looked at me and smiled.

"It's always about a boy," she said. "That's why I never got married. Do I know who he is?"

I cleared my throat. Was it me, or was the room getting hotter?

"He was in your class last semester," I said to Ms. Miller, who was staring at me intently. "I was supposed to get together with him this semester, but he didn't come back to school."

"Are you talking about Kyle?"

When I heard Kyle's name, I nearly fell out of the chair. How did Ms. Miller know?

"How did you know?" I asked Ms. Miller. "Did Kyle say something to you?"

Now I was the one who was asking the questions.

"You have good choice in men," Ms. Miller said to me with a wink. "Kyle did not say anything to me, but I kind of put two and two together. He was one of my better students last semester. In fact, he gave me that poster right over there of LeBron James. I was so sad to hear that he wouldn't be coming back."

Hearing Ms. Miller speak so highly of Kyle brought a smile to my face but also made me miss him even more.

"At least I know that this isn't about my teaching ability," Ms. Miller said jokingly. "Give it time, Sandy. You're too good a student to let something like this bring you down."

I got up and thanked Ms. Miller for meeting with me. I was about to walk out the door when I remembered why I had come here.

"What about my paper?" I turned and said to Ms. Miller.

Ms. Miller looked at me and said, "Isn't it obvious?"

I looked at the picture of LeBron, and then I looked at Ms. Miller who was smiling at me.

"Last year, Kyle wrote his paper about his roommate, who he really looked up to. Why don't you write your paper about Kyle?"

Ms. Miller was right. I was going to write about my true love, even if he doesn't even know it. I thanked Ms. Miller and headed back to the dorm.

As I began walking through campus, only then did it hit me. What did I get myself into now?

Chester, I Need Your Help

I arrived at my dorm room hoping to find Chester with Maria. To my surprise, neither of them was there. Then I remembered they were going to the mall. I decided to start on my paper. I must've sat there for nearly forty-five minutes without writing down a single word. It's ironic how little I actually knew about Kyle. *This is going to be impossible*, I thought. Just then, Chester and Maria returned from the mall. It was so cute how Chester carried all of Maria's bags for her. I wondered if Kyle would do the same for me. I turned to Chester, who was putting down Maria's bags.

"Chester, do you remember the paper that Kyle did of you?"

"How did you know about that?" Chester replied.

"Ms. Miller told me about it. What can you tell me about the paper?" Chester looked at me with a funny look.

"To tell you the truth, Sandy, I never read it. He just interviewed me and did it all by himself. It must've been really good because he got an 'A' on it. Why do you ask?"

"Well," I said gloomily, "I think that I'm going to be doing my paper on Kyle. Only problem is I really don't know much of anything about him."

"Hmmmm," Chester replied in his usual Chester tone. "I guess you could interview me also. I am the resident expert on Kyle. You know, Sandy, you could also just call him."

I had not thought of that. The thought of calling him intrigued me greatly. Then I began to wonder if Kyle even thought of me anymore. Maybe he had already found his true love. How could I justify just calling him out of the blue, no less doing my semester paper on him?

I turned to Chester and said, "No, I don't want to call him. I think it may be awkward."

"Cheer up," Chester said, smiling. "We will help you get this done. What have you got so far?"

I held up my blank paper to Chester, and we all started to laugh. It felt good to laugh again. I couldn't even remember the last time that I genuinely laughed since returning to school.

"Write down a bunch of questions, and when you're ready, you can interview me," Chester smiled at said. "But first, let's go eat dinner. I'm starving."

I was feeling a little hungry for once, and knowing that Chester would help me with my paper really helped to put me at ease. I grabbed my coat, and we headed to the cafeteria for dinner. I wished Kyle was with us, and again, I was sad.

A Change in Plans

How can I write a paper about someone that I hardly knew even with the help of his former roommate? Maybe what I should ask myself is how I fell in love with someone that I hardly knew. *I'll never finish this paper*, I thought. At least when Kyle did his paper on Chester, he had access to Chester.

I must have sat there for about an hour when it finally hit me. I am not going to do my paper on Kyle. I am going to do my paper on "true love." Of course, Kyle will be the basis for the paper, but nobody needs to know that.

I turned to Maria and said, "Hey, Maria, what can you tell me about true love?"

Maria gave me a dumbfounded look. "What kind of question is that?"

What was I thinking asking Maria about true love? I needed to ask that question of someone who is already in love. So I made a list of all the people that I knew who have found true love, at least in my opinion. Of course, my mother was number 1 on the list; number 2 was my aunt June and uncle Wayne. They have been married for over thirty years, and they were always together. I added a few more friends and relatives to the list. Now all I had to do was ask them about true love and what it means to them.

Just then, Chester came down to our room.

"Did you finish your questions, Sandy?" he asked me, trying to impress Maria.

I looked at Maria, who rolled her eyes at me. *Chester could be a pain in the butt on occasion, but he only wants to help*, I thought.

"I decided to take another approach, Chester. I am not going to do my paper on Kyle."

I could tell that my reply caught Chester by surprise and probably hurt his feelings a little as well.

"I decided that I am not qualified to write a paper on Kyle, Chester. Instead, I am going to do my paper on true love."

Now it was Chester's turn to roll his eyes. I don't blame him; after all, what suddenly made me an expert on true love?

Then Chester said, "All I can say, Sandy, is good luck. But if you ever need my help, do not be afraid to ask."

What a good friend Chester was, I thought. I hope that Maria realized what a great guy she has. Chester kissed Maria on the cheek and headed back to his room. I decided that tomorrow I will start contacting the people on my list.

I looked over at Maria who was half asleep, trying to finish reading her psychology chapter.

"Maria!" I yelled causing her to jump.

"Huh?" Maria muttered, half asleep.

"Do you think that Kyle still thinks about me?" I asked her.

Maria sat up and rubbed her eyes.

"Yes, Sandy, I do believe that he thinks of you a lot. Don't give up hope. You just need to believe."

Maria's words of encouragement really made me feel better. I did believe that, one day, Kyle and I will be together. Maybe it would happen tonight in my dreams.

I really felt good about the direction that I was taking my paper. I hope that Ms. Miller would feel the same way. I was exhausted. As soon as my head hit the pillow, I was asleep.

The Paper

What is true love? How could someone who has never experienced true love write a paper on true love? Of all the people that I talked to about true love, my mom was the most helpful. I really enjoyed her story of how she played hard to get on purpose so Dad would give her more attention and how she cried when Dad left her to join the military. Hearing her stories made me realize how much they really loved each other. When Dad died, it was though a part of her died also. But through it all, she really did experience true love.

Aunt June and Uncle Wayne were also very helpful. They had been married for over twenty-five years and were pretty much inseparable. But they were not high school sweethearts. They met after college. Some friends set them up on a blind date, and their first date did not go very well. It seemed that Uncle Wayne got drunk and threw up all over Aunt June's clothes. Uncle Wayne felt so bad that he bought her a new outfit and proceeded to sweep Aunt June off her feet.

In time, I did manage to gather a lot of good material, but it was all secondhand material. I wanted to somehow put in my twist on true love, but let's face it, I was not an expert. I didn't just want to write a paper about true love; I wanted to write the paper about true love through my own eyes. But how could I do that? I went to lie down on my bed, and before I knew it, I was asleep.

As I was sleeping, I had a dream. In my dream, Kyle and I were holding hands, walking through the park. Kyle asked me if I had found true love.

"Yes," I said to him. "You are my true love. You have always been my true love. And you will always be my true love."

I woke up with the dream still very fresh in my mind. Even though it was just a dream, the feeling that I had at that moment was unlike anything else that I had felt before. That's when I realized that true love isn't something you can just write a paper about. It was more than that. It was a feeling that no words can describe. It was something that is so powerful and unique to each relationship that it can never be duplicated.

I wrote my entire paper that night. I did not mention anyone's name; I didn't need to. This paper was about love as seen through my own eyes and my interpretation of what love means to me and what I expect from love.

As I finished my story, this was my final paragraph:

> What do I know about true love? Probably not more than the next person. What I do know is that I want to find true love, I want to feel true love, and I want to be in love. Although I have yet to experience this feeling, I am in no hurry. I will not chase it, nor should I have to wait for it. When it happens, I will know, and so will the person who shares this experience with me. It is the culmination of two people who decide to share an entire lifetime with each other unconditionally. This is true love as seen through my eyes. One day, I hope to feel it through my heart.

Not bad, I thought. Hopefully, Ms. Miller would feel the same way.

The Reaction

Even though my paper wasn't due for another month, I decided to turn it into Ms. Miller early. I was very happy with the way it turned out, and I figured that Ms. Miller wouldn't read it until she got the other papers in anyway. I was wrong.

I gave my paper to Ms. Miller before class started on Tuesday. She gave me a surprised look but took the paper and thanked me.

Today before class, Ms. Miller asked me to meet her to discuss the paper. *Oh my god*, I thought. Did she not like the paper? Did I do it wrong? She told me to meet her at her office later today after my last class. I had no idea why, and I started to feel really nervous.

Maria and Chester decided to meet me for lunch today at the campus center. It was a good thing too. I needed to tell them about Ms. Miller and my paper. Maria was already at the sandwich shop, saving a table for us. She waved to me and called me over.

"Where's Chester?" I asked her.

Chester had a very bad habit of forgetting his wallet, and Maria would often end up footing the bill.

"It's not like he's poor," Maria said shaking her head.

I just sat there and smiled. Then I saw my chance.

"Maria, Ms. Miller wants me to meet her later today to talk about my paper."

"What?" Maria said out loud. "You mean she read it already?"

"Apparently," I replied. "I wonder if she didn't like it. I am really worried, Maria."

Just then, Chester arrived, waving his wallet to us.

"Sorry," Chester said sheepishly, "my treat today."

Maria told Chester about Ms. Miller wanting to speak to me about my paper. Chester shrugged his shoulders and said, "Maybe you need to do it again."

Maria slapped Chester in the shoulder and said, "You stop that. This is serious."

Actually, I really had no idea why Ms. Miller wanted to meet with me to discuss my paper. I was really happy with it, and it would really be a bummer if she asked me to do it again. I did not mention Kyle's name at all in my paper. The paper was about "true love" as seen through my eyes, and no one needed to know that it was about Kyle.

"Do you want me to go with you?" Maria said.

"No, that's okay," I said. "This has nothing to do with you."

I really appreciated Maria wanting to be there for me. All semester, Maria and Chester had been the glue that has held me together. Without them, I would pretty much be lost. I began to wonder how this semester would've been had Kyle come back to school. Would we be together right now? Would we be in love? Will we ever be together? I never had so much uncertainty in my life until now, and for the first time, it was getting the best of me.

Meeting Ms. Miller Again

Well, it was time, time for my meeting with Ms. Miller. Not knowing was absolutely killing me, but at the same time, I was afraid to find out.

As usual, Ms. Miller was busy grading papers, but she seemed to know that I was there. Before I could even knock on her door, she smiled and said to me, "Come in, Sandy."

I walked in to her office and sat down on the chair across from her. I couldn't even look her in the eye. I didn't know what to say or do. I just sat there staring at her desk.

"Do you know why I called you in to see me, Sandy?" Ms. Miller asked, breaking the silence.

I shrugged my shoulders and said, "No, Ms. Miller," still not making eye contact.

"The reason I called you in Sandy is because of your paper."

Okay, here it comes, I thought. She's going to tell me how bad it was, how I didn't do it right, how I will need to do it again. "Just tell me already," I wanted to yell out to her. That was why what she told me next completely blew me away.

"Sandy," she said solemnly. "In all my years of teaching, I've lived by two codes. The first one is to never fool around with any student or fellow teacher. That is self-explanatory as you might expect. My second code is never to get involved or interfere in a student's life. Sandy, for the first time, I am about to break one of my codes."

I finally looked up at Ms. Miller. I saw genuineness in her eyes that told me to trust her and listen to what she had to say. Ms. Miller smiled at me, and I smiled back.

"Sandy, this paper is about Kyle, isn't it?"

I nodded and said yes.

"When I read your paper last night, Sandy, it made me cry. You say that you want to find true love, feel true love, and be in love. Sandy, you have already found it. You are already feeling it. Sandy, let's face it, you are in love."

I sat there and smiled. Somehow I knew. I knew it from the first time I saw Kyle, and I knew it when we said goodbye to each other last semester. Tears started to run down my face. I always knew.

Ms. Miller got up from her desk and walked toward the poster that Kyle had given her. "You know what you have to do, Sandy," she said, touching the poster.

I gave Ms. Miller a confused look. "Please tell me," I said to her.

"Sandy, you need to go to him. True love doesn't always come to those who wait. Sometimes you have to create your own destiny. Sometimes you need to 'just do it.'"

Ms. Miller was right. For once in my life, I was going to do something totally crazy. I got up and gave Ms. Miller a hug. *Boy, does she smell good,* I thought.

"Spring break is coming up, Sandy. Go find your true love."

I left Ms. Miller's office full of determination, and then it hit me. I couldn't do this alone. I would need a lot of help.

The Plan

When I got back to my dorm room, Chester and Maria were already there, waiting for me. I barely had a chance to put my backpack down when the first question came from Maria, "Well, are you going to make us ask?"

"Well," I said, stalling for time until I figured out what I wanted to say.

"C'mon, Sandy, spill the beans. What did Ms. Miller say?"

"Well," I said again. "She did read my paper, and I guess she really liked it a lot."

"That's it?" Chester blurted out.

"Well, not quite," I said with a wry smile. "According to Ms. Miller, I don't need to find true love. According to her, I am already in love."

"Duh," Chester said sarcastically, "tell us something we don't know."

Maria gave Chester a dirty look and told him to behave. Then she asked, "Did she say anything else to you?"

"Well," I said for the umpteenth time. "She says that I should go to him."

Chester jumped to his feet, pumped his fist in the air, and shouted, "Road trip!"

"I just don't think that I can do it, Chester," I said to him sadly.

"Of course, you can," Maria interrupted. "We'll go with you."

It's so good when you have friends who can read your mind. I didn't even have to ask them to go with me. Chester figured it out, and by bus, it would take us about twelve hours to get to Kyle. Chester even said that he would pay for the tickets.

"I guess he's not always cheap," Maria whispered to me.

"I will call Kyle tomorrow and tell him about our plans," Chester said. "He will be so happy to see us."

"Wait, Chester," I interrupted. "I want to surprise Kyle. I don't want him to know that I am coming. Just in case he already found someone, he won't have to see me cry."

I could tell that Chester was very excited to go see Kyle. But before I commit to this trip, I needed to speak to one more person, my mother. I asked Chester and Maria to leave the room so I could speak to her in private. I wasn't sure how Mom would take this, and part of me was afraid to tell her the reason why I wasn't coming home for spring break. I just hope that she understands.

"Hi, Mom," I said nervously.

"Hi, Sandy," she said back happily.

"Mom, I need to talk to you about something."

"Is there anything wrong?" my mother asked.

I told my mom about how sad I have been since learning that Kyle wouldn't be returning to school. I told her how unhappy I was at school and how my grades have dropped because of it. I told her about my paper about true love. I told her what Ms. Miller said to me about my paper and about myself. Through it all, Mom did not say a single word. Then I told her what Ms. Miller said I should do. I was fully prepared for her to tell me what a fool I was, but instead, she shocked me by asking me something that I never expected to hear.

"Sandy, is he the one?" my mother said solemnly.

"Yes, Mother, Kyle is the one."

For a brief moment, the phone was silent. Then my mom said, "Sandy, if he is the one, then you go to him."

"Oh, Mom, I love you," I said to her excitedly.

"I love you too, Sandy," Mom said, her voice cracking.

I ran out of the dorm room to go look for Maria and Chester. When they saw me running to them, they already knew.

"Road trip!" the two of them yelled in unison.

For the first time all semester, I felt alive again. I couldn't wait for spring break to arrive.

Road Trip

Today is the day. It is finally here. Tonight at 9:00 p.m., we leave to go see Kyle. These last two weeks have dragged on like two months. You don't know how many times I have talked myself out of doing this over the past two weeks. Everything has been set up by Chester. Kyle is expecting to see Chester and Maria. He has no idea that I will be accompanying them. I want to surprise Kyle, but I am hoping that Kyle doesn't have a surprise for me. For all I know, he could already be with someone. I wouldn't expect him to wait for me; he has no obligation to do so.

Just then, Maria woke up. "What time is it?" she said, rubbing her eyes.

"It's about six thirty," I told her.

"What? Are you crazy?" Maria said sarcastically.

Maria was right. I probably was a little crazy. I couldn't sleep a wink last night. I must have gotten up about thirty times last night to check the time. Maria put her head back down and quickly fell back asleep. I was tired. I decided to try to go back to sleep as well.

After lying down for about twenty minutes, I decided to get out of bed and go take a shower. The dorm was pretty empty. Most of the students had gone home for spring break, and only a few people remained. I decided to stay downstairs in the lounge and read a book. Before I knew it, I fell asleep. I had a dream that I was outside Kyle's house. I knocked on the door, and a young woman carrying a baby answered the door.

"Do I know you?" the woman asked me.

"No," I answered sadly and walked away. The dream was so disturbing that I actually woke up. I went back upstairs to my room and told Maria about my dream.

"Do you think it means anything?" I asked Maria.

"It just means you're crazy," Maria said, smiling. "But we already knew that."

We decided to go to the mall. I wanted to get something for Kyle. I wasn't sure what would be appropriate. I was confident that I could figure it out. Also, I wanted to kill time and make this day go by faster. Chester joined us, and we were off.

We got back from the mall a little later than I wanted to. Now we really had to scramble to make sure that we got to the bus stop on time. Arriving at the bus stop, we picked up our tickets and boarded our bus. The bus was only about half full and departed the station on time. I was so exhausted that I fell asleep in no time.

We made a couple of rest stops along the way. On the second stop, we decided to get breakfast from a nearby McDonald's. The last leg of the trip would be another three hours. We would arrive in Kyle's town at around 9:00 a.m.

As the bus departed for the last leg, I suddenly became very nervous. I began asking myself, *Am I prepared to deal with what I might find?* To be honest, I couldn't answer. *It was too late to turn back anyway,* I thought. I took out the gift I bought for Kyle. I hope that I get the chance to give it to him. I hope that I will find my true love.

Arrival

I must've dozed off. I didn't even realize that we were here. It was a gloomy morning, overcast with a light drizzle. Then out of nowhere, Chester jumped out of his seat and yelled, "Look! It's Kyle's store."

I quickly turned to see if I could catch a glimpse of Kyle, but the bus was going too fast. *Too bad the bus couldn't just drop us off right here,* I thought. We continued on for another few miles before we hit the bus stop. We got off the bus and waited for our bags. I was a nervous wreck. Part of me wanted to hop back on the bus and go back home. I went into the ladies' room to try to freshen up. Of course, I wanted to look good for Kyle, but at this point in time, there was only so much that I could do. Chester brought our bags to a curb and proceeded to flag down a taxi. *This was it,* I thought. *My entire life comes down to this one fleeting moment.*

When we told the taxicab driver where we wanted to go, he asked why. Chester told him that it was to visit a friend. As we drove over to Kyle's store, the rain started to drop a little harder. I hope that this wasn't an omen. Normally, I was not a very superstitious person, but today I needed all the luck that I can get.

We pulled into the parking lot of Kyle's store. Chester paid the man and told me the plan. He would go into the store first with Maria. They entered the store together. I slipped in after them and waited in an empty aisle. This way, I could hear everything.

Chester and Maria walked toward the front counter. Rob was sitting by the cash register, reading the paper. He saw Chester approaching and put the paper down. "Can I help you?" he said kindly.

"Hi, I'm Chester, and this is Maria. We are both friends of Kyle from school."

"Oh," Rob said with a big smile. "He's been expecting you. Let me call him from the office."

Rob walked to the back and quickly came back with Kyle.

Kyle came out with a big smile on his face. "Oh my god," he screamed. "It's my brother from another mother!"

Kyle and Chester embraced. I almost thought that they were going to kiss each other. Then Kyle gave Maria a hug. He looked great, so happy and full of life.

He and Chester continued to talk for a few minutes when Chester said, "Hey, Kyle, there's a customer over there who needs some help."

"I'll go," Rob said quickly.

"No," Chester quickly stopped Rob. "I think Kyle should go. I want to see him in action."

Kyle punched Chester in the arm and with a big smile walked toward me. I had the hood of my parka over my head and turned away from him so he couldn't see my face.

"Excuse me, miss," Kyle said in a voice that made my heart sink. "Can I help you with anything?"

I just stood there. I was too nervous to say anything.

Kyle tapped me on the shoulder, "Hey, miss, can I help you?"

This time, I turned around and removed my hood. Our eyes met in unison. Kyle took a step back but did not say a word. "What do you think of ObamaCare?" I asked him with a smile. *Oh my god*, I thought to myself, but just like that, the ice was broken.

What Now?

I just stood there staring at Sandy. I couldn't believe that she was here in my store. My dad, who was watching the whole thing, came up to us just in the nick of time.

"Anyone I should meet, son?" he said with a smile.

"Ummm, this is Sandy. Sandy, my father." Oh my god, I was really pressuring.

"Nice to finally meet you, Sandy. I've heard a lot about you," my dad said, still smiling.

"Nice to meet you too, sir," Sandy said, smiling also. "You have a very nice store here."

My dad put his arm around me and said, "Thanks to this guy. We are doing really well these days."

The store was doing much better although it is debatable whether I had that much to do with it. I just kept staring at Sandy. My heart was beating like a taiko drum on steroids. She was as radiant and beautiful as I remembered her. Sandy's eyes caught me staring at her, and I quickly turned away.

"Hi, I'm Chester," Chester blurted, obviously feeling left out. "And this is my girlfriend, Maria."

"Nice to meet both of you," my dad said shaking both of their hands. "How long will you be in town?"

"Maybe a couple of days," Maria said.

"Where are you staying?" my dad said, obviously carrying the conversation for me.

"We were just going to get a room at one of the local motels," Chester said. "We haven't figured that part out yet."

"Don't be silly," my dad said. "We have plenty of room at our house."

I looked at my dad, who was looking at me kind of funny. I can't believe that Sandy will be in my house. I still stood there, not saying anything. Sandy looked at me and also gave me a funny look. I don't think that my reaction was what she expected.

Don't get me wrong, I was very happy to see Sandy, but for the first time in my life, I felt like I had no idea how to handle this situation.

"Why don't you kids go into town and catch up," my dad said, bringing me back to reality. "Rob and I can hold down the fort for one day. Just be back in time for dinner. I think that Mother will prepare a special feast for tonight."

As we walked out of the store, Sandy gave me a sad smile. I smiled back, and she looked away. Chester and Maria, on the other hand, were giggling and laughing like little kids on a field trip. I could tell that Sandy was disappointed in me. I didn't even give her a hug. *What am I doing?* I thought.

We got into my car. Sandy sat in the front seat next to me while Chester and Maria sat in the back. As we drove off, we did not say a word to each other. Maybe you can't go home again. I was totally confused, and true love was the farthest thing from my mind.

The Mall

We drove to the local mall to go and have lunch. The girls sat down at the table while Chester and I went to the men's room. As soon as we walked in, Chester knew that something was wrong.

"Are you okay?" Chester asked me. "I thought you would be happy to see us, especially Sandy."

Dang, Chester, he was too perceptive for his own good. I turned away from him and looked at myself in the mirror. I didn't like what I saw.

"You know, Chester," I said looking back at him. "I'm not sure what is wrong with me. I am glad to see all of you, of course, but I am worried. What if Sandy is not my true love? How will I know in such a short period? What if we made a mistake?"

"Dude," Chester said with a smirk, "quit analyzing and just be yourself. Stop worrying about things that you cannot control. If it was meant to be, then it will happen. If it wasn't, you move on."

Chester was right as usual. Honestly, part of me missed him more than I missed Sandy. We did our business and went back to our table. Maria and Sandy were sitting there, laughing about something. It was good to see Sandy laugh. I sat down next to her and did something totally unexpected. I reached under the table and grabbed Sandy's hand. She looked at me surprised, and then she smiled. I smiled back at her, and she took my hand in both of her hands. Her hands were so soft and warm, and a tingle went through my entire body.

We ate lunch and cruised around the mall for a while. Sandy and I walked hand in hand the entire way. We walked by a jewelry store and stopped to look at the diamonds. Chester walked beside me and nudged my arm and laughed. I pointed to Maria who also seemed very fascinated with the sparkling gems and laughed back.

As we continued to walk, I could feel myself letting go. I still couldn't believe that I was holding hands with Sandy in my hometown mall. When they came to the hardware store earlier in the morning, I think that they caught me a bit off guard. *Just go with the flow*, I thought. *Just be myself.*

As we drove to my house, Sandy fell asleep. She seemed so much more at peace than she was earlier in the morning. I blamed myself for that. Even asleep, she looked so beautiful. Chester and Maria also fell asleep. I took this opportunity to call my mom and give her a heads-up. She said that she already knew and that Kevin was very excited to meet my friends.

Meeting the Family

As I pulled into my driveway, Kevin was already outside, waving and yelling. He was yelling so loud that he managed to wake up everyone who was asleep in the car. We had a fairly large house with lots of room for everyone. As we entered the house, Kevin lead the way, screaming, "Kyle and his friends are here," at the top of his little lungs.

"Welcome," my mom said with a smile.

I introduced her to my friends, saving Sandy for last.

"So you're the one who has my son all tied up in knots. I can see why."

Sandy just smiled shyly and looked at me. We made eye contact, and I winked back at her.

"Kyle, why don't you take them upstairs and let them get washed up? I hear you all had quite a long trip."

We proceeded to walk upstairs followed by Kevin, until my mother called him back to help her in the kitchen. I turned to my mom, who smiled at me and nodded her head approvingly.

I took Chester and Maria upstairs to our guest room. Maria decided to take a shower while Chester decided to take a nap.

"Do you want to rest also?" I said to Sandy.

"What are you going to do, Kyle?" she replied.

"I don't know," I said shrugging my shoulders. "Did you want to do anything in particular?"

Sandy looked at me and smiled. "I just want to be with you. That's all I want to do."

Just then, Kevin came running upstairs, spoiling the mood like only he can.

"Kyle," he yelled, "let's go play outside."

His timing couldn't have been more impeccable.

"I'm a little busy," I said to Kevin. "I want to spend time with my friends."

Kevin looked at me and then looked at Chester.

"But he's asleep," he said, pointing at Chester.

Just then, Sandy jumped in. "Let's go outside, Kevin. Kyle and I will take you."

I looked at Sandy, who was smiling at me. My heart was already beginning to melt each time she looked at me. I wanted so much to be alone with her, but I knew that time would come.

Outside, Kevin got our baseball gloves and the baseball. When Sandy saw this, she asked Kevin, "Do you have a glove for me?"

Kevin ran back into the garage and came out with my father's old glove. He gave it to Sandy, who put it on and immediately called for the ball. Kevin wasn't the best thrower, and he uncorked a wild one that bounced and skidded toward Sandy. I quickly ran behind her to retrieve the ball, but out of nowhere, she snagged the ball on one hop and quickly threw it back to Kevin.

"Whoa," Kevin cried. "That was awesome."

Sandy then turned around to me in time to notice the amazed look on my face.

"Three years on the hot corner for my softball team," she said confidently. "Can you tell?"

The more I learned about her, the more I wanted to know. I remembered that day when she left me at school, how she told me if I ever find true love to not let it go. I still couldn't believe that she was here with me. I watched in amazement how graceful she was, how good of an athlete she was. I began to wonder, *Could she be the one?*

Dinner

I could tell that my mom was preparing quite the feast. She spent all afternoon in the kitchen. Sandy and Maria both offered to help her, but she politely told them that she has everything under control. Sandy decided to take a nap, and Kevin set the dining room table.

I decided to check in on my mom and see what she was making. Whatever it was, it smelled really good. My mom was busy peeling potatoes, and I decided to help her. I could tell that something was on her mind, so I decided to find out.

"Well?" I said. "I know that something is on your mind."

My mom put down her peeler and said, "You know that she loves you."

I looked at my mom and said, "Don't be silly."

"Kyle, I'm a woman. I think I know. For her to come all this way and take a chance on seeing you. Also, I can see it in her eyes."

I did not say a word. I just sat there, thinking about what my mother had just said. Just then, Dad came home. He walked through the garage door and gave my mother a kiss. He then grabbed a beer from the fridge and sat down at the table next to me.

"Well?" he said, smiling at me.

Before I could even say anything, my mom beat me to the punch. "I think that someone is in love," she said, giggling like a little girl.

My dad looked at me and smiled. "Is that right, Kyle?"

I could feel myself turning bright red. And to make matters worse, I really didn't have anything to say. I just sat there and smiled.

My mom looked at my dad and said, "Do you remember when you came home to me?"

My dad just smiled; now it was his turn to blush. "Yes, I remember," he said sheepishly. "I also remember your dad nearly shooting me."

Mom and Dad laughed. My dad got up and headed to his room to get washed up for dinner. I looked at my mom and said, "Grandpa almost shot Dad?"

My mother laughed and told me how Dad came to see her at her house and fell asleep. When he woke up, he forgot where he was and stumbled over a chair, looking for the bathroom. The next thing she remembered was her dad running out with his shotgun yelling, "Burglar, burglar!" Luckily for my dad, he turned on the lights before he shot.

"Your father had a big cut on his forehead, and Grandpa used to brag about how he taught your father a lesson," my mom said laughing. "Why don't you go upstairs and tell your friends that dinner is almost ready?"

I headed upstairs where Sandy was sleeping on my bed. She looked so beautiful lying there. I tapped her on the shoulder to wake her up. She rolled onto her back and looked at me and smiled.

"Sometimes dreams do come true," she said, gazing into my eyes. "But if I am dreaming, please don't ever wake me up."

Dinner

After many hours of preparation, our dinner was finally ready. I called Chester, Maria, and Sandy to come downstairs for supper. Chester of course was the first one down, drawing a sarcastic comment from Maria. We all gathered around the table, and of course, my mother volunteered me to say grace. I gave my mom a dirty look, and I asked everyone at the table to join hands.

"Dear Lord, bless this food that we are about to receive. Please bless my friends who have journeyed a long way to bless us with their presence. I would like to say more Lord, but I'm sure that you can understand how hungry Chester is. Amen."

We dug into Mom's pot roast and mashed potatoes like there was no tomorrow. Everyone gave her cooking rave reviews, and I could tell that this made my mom very happy. For dessert, she baked one of her awesome apple pies. It was nice to see my friends and my parents talk to each other like they were old friends. They were especially intrigued with Chester's sudden rise to riches and about life in Hawaii. I reached under the table and offered my hand to Sandy, who took my hand immediately. This caught the attention of Kevin, who felt the need to announce to the table what we were doing.

"Oh, Kevin," my mom jumped in. "Be happy for your brother."

"I don't think holding a girl's hand would make me happy," Kevin muttered back.

My mom took my dad's hand, and Chester took Maria's hand also. Kevin crossed his arms, looked at everyone, and said, "I'm going to go play video games now. May I be excused?"

We all laughed at Kevin and continued to talk for another hour. I could tell that everyone was getting tired; after all, it was a long day. Sandy and Maria went into the kitchen to help my mom clean up. Chester went to see what Kevin was playing and quickly jumped in. I went upstairs and prepared everyone's bedding. Chester would sleep in Kevin's room, and the girls would sleep in my room. Kevin would sleep with my parents, and I would sleep on the floor in the family room upstairs.

Soon it was time for everyone to sleep. After saying "good night" to everyone, we all went our separate ways. I was so exhausted that I fell asleep in no time. I was sound asleep when I felt something against me. "Kevin, go away," I muttered, half asleep.

"Do you really want me to go?" said a soft and gentle voice.

Oh my god, it was Sandy. I turned to make sure that it was really her. We made eye contact, and she smiled. For the first time, I realized that Sandy was here for me and that she wanted to be with me. It was like I died and went to heaven.

The Best Night of My Life

I turned to face Sandy. Her silhouette in the moonlight was breathtaking. *Oh my god*, I thought, *I hope I don't have morning breath.* Everyone else was sleeping; it was just the two of us. For the first time since she arrived, we were all alone, and I really didn't know what to do. I was going to ask Sandy about her thoughts on ObamaCare, but after further review, I decided not to. Luckily for me, Sandy broke the ice.

"So, Kyle, you never told me. Are you happy to see me?"

Sandy was right, I never told her thank-you for coming to see me. She took all the risk in coming here. Right at that moment, I had feelings going through me that I had never felt before. I sat up looking down at Sandy's eyes. I could see uncertainty in her eyes. I needed to do something that would show her how I felt about her.

"Sandy," I said softly, "close your eyes."

Sandy closed her eyes. And then I kissed her. As I lifted away from her, she slowly opened her eyes; a tear ran down the side of her face.

"What's wrong?" I asked. "Did I do something wrong?"

Sandy looked at me as more tears flowed down her face. "No, Kyle. Everything is perfect."

Sandy sat up, and we kissed some more. I wiped the tears away from her face and smiled. I could feel myself letting go. I had put my family before myself, and in doing so, I really had to keep all of my feelings for Sandy in check. But now that she was here with me, I didn't want to hold back any longer. I pulled Sandy toward me, and we embraced. *Boy, does she smell good*, I thought.

"Sandy," I whispered into her ear. "When you showed up at the store today, I really didn't know how to react. I was happy of course, but part of me was not sure if I would ever see you again. I made a choice to help my family, and with that choice came sacrifices."

Sandy looked at me with understanding eyes. "And now that I'm here?" she asked.

"Now that you are here, Sandy, it's like all the feelings for you that I tried to hide have broken through the gates of my mind. I can no longer hold back these feelings. I need to just let them go and follow them wherever they take me."

"Kyle, when I found out that you weren't coming back to school, I was devastated. I didn't want to be there anymore. I began to doubt whether we would ever be together. But through it all, I could never get you out of my mind. That's why I decided to come here. I had to know whether we had a chance, whether you and I would ever be together."

I put my hands around Sandy's cheeks and lifted her face toward me. "Sandy, you had me at ObamaCare."

We started to laugh, and just like that, any tension that was left had suddenly disappeared.

We continued to talk all night long. After all, we really didn't know all that much about each other. We talked about our childhood, our wishes, and our dreams. We talked about sports and Ms. Miller. We even talked about ObamaCare for god's sake. Before we knew it, the sun was coming out. The greatest night of my life was turning into the greatest time of my life.

The Next Morning

I woke up to find myself all alone. I began to wonder if last night was a just a dream. I got up to see if anyone else was awake. I could hear my mom cooking breakfast downstairs and my dad talking to her while probably drinking his coffee. I went to check on Sandy. She was sound asleep in my room with Maria. I went downstairs to talk to my dad and see if there was anything special that needed to be done at the store.

My mom handed me a cup of coffee and said, "Good morning."

My mom had that look in her eye. I knew that she had something to say to me. I looked at my dad, who smiled and looked away.

Then it came. "You know, Kyle," my mom said in her typical mom's-always-right tone. "I think Sandy is a keeper. What do you think Papa?"

My dad just smiled at me and said to my mom, "You know, dear, I think Kyle can figure that out for himself."

This was new territory for me. It was as though my childhood had just ended, and I was all grown up now. I reminded myself that this was the choice that I made when I decided to come back and work at the store. Then it hit me. Sandy will be leaving tomorrow to go back to school. I think that we're together, but are we?

I could hear someone making noise upstairs and went back up to see who it was. It was Sandy.

"I came out to be with you, but you were gone," she said smiling.

I guess last night wasn't a dream, I thought and gave Sandy a big hug. She gave me a kiss, and I began to wonder if I had morning breath. Just about then, Chester came out, scratching his head and some other part of his anatomy.

"Ahem," I said to Chester who immediately stopped scratching. "Did you sleep well, dude?"

"Oh, man," Chester said, rubbing his eyes, "Kevin's bed was a bit small."

Sandy and I both laughed, prompting Maria to wake up.

"What do you guys want to do today?" I asked them.

Not surprisingly, no one answered. *Oh well*, I thought, *I guess we'll figure it out as we go along.* Then to my surprise, Sandy took my arm and whispered to me, "I'll go anywhere that you go."

Then my mom called up to us from downstairs, "Come and eat, kids."

We all headed downstairs to the dining room. There were pancakes, bacon, eggs, sausage, and hash browns and lots of everything.

"What are you kids planning to do today?" my mom asked my friends.

Not surprisingly, no one answered again.

"I think I am going to take them to the lake today," I said to my mom.

"It should be really nice there today," my dad said before taking a sip of coffee.

My mom looked at my dad and said, "Why don't we barbecue for dinner tonight?"

"That's a great idea," my dad said. "I'll go and pick up some steaks and brats."

After breakfast, we all headed upstairs and got ready to go to the lake. Sandy gave me a kiss before heading into the bathroom. *One more day*, I thought, *and then she'll be gone again.*

The Lake

The lake was about forty-five minutes away from my house. It was small as lakes go but very beautiful. We packed a picnic lunch with some sandwiches and a cooler of drinks. It felt really good having Sandy ride shotgun with me. Every minute that we spent together just felt so natural. It was like a perfect fit.

As we got to the lake, I noticed that some high school friends of mine were there. I pulled up next to them to say hi. They were getting ready to play some volleyball and invited us to join them. I turned around and looked at Chester, who looked the other way. Chester wasn't the greatest athlete, and I could tell that he didn't want to embarrass himself. Maria was pretty much like Chester, so I didn't even bother to ask her.

When I looked at Sandy, she gave me a high five and said, "Let's go, babe."

When I introduced Sandy to my friends, I introduced her as a friend of mine from college. I could tell that this irritated Sandy, who gave me an elbow to the gut. I guess I wasn't used to saying that I have a girlfriend yet.

We split the teams up, and Sandy insisted that she wanted to be on the same team as "her friend from college." I played volleyball in high school, but I was never really very good. As we started playing, I was amazed at how athletic and graceful Sandy was.

She was everywhere, digging balls and setting up the others on our team for kills. With Sandy's help, we killed the other team.

As we shook hands after the game, one of my buddies came up to me and said, "Gee, Kyle, I didn't know that you were going to bring a ringer with you."

I turned around and looked at Sandy, and then I turned back to my buddy and said, "That ringer is my girlfriend."

Sandy heard this and started to laugh. She came up to me, put her arms around me, and gave me a kiss. Then she said, "And don't you forget it."

We hung out with my friends for the rest of the afternoon. Sandy got along really well with everyone. Chester and Maria made new friends as well. It was getting late, and soon it was time for us to drive back home. We said our goodbye to my friends, and some of them asked Sandy when she was going to come back. Sandy shrugged her shoulders and then looked at me. I didn't say anything, and I could tell that this disappointed her.

As we walked back to my car, Sandy whispered into my ear, "I haven't even left, and I'm already starting to miss you."

I had to look away. I didn't want Sandy to see the tear falling from my eye.

Our Last Night

By the time we got back home, dinner was already waiting for us. My mom and dad prepared a feast fit for a king and all of his court. There were steaks, hamburgers, hot dogs, fried chicken, pretty much every type of food known to man. I was pleasantly surprised to see my grandparents at the house also. I introduced Sandy and my friends to them. My grandmother gave Sandy a hug, while my grandfather gave me a wink and a thumbs-up.

After washing up, it was time to eat. Everyone gathered around the dining room table, and to my surprise, Sandy volunteered to say grace. We all joined hands around the table, and Sandy began to speak.

"Dear Lord, please bless this food that we are about to receive. It is truly a blessing to be in the company of such a wonderful family and great friends at this dinner table. Lord, continue to guide us in your infinite wisdom, and thank you so much for bringing us together on this joyous night. Amen."

We dug in, and we dug deep. I was starving, and Chester seemed to inhale his food. I don't even think that he came up for air.

"What time are you leaving tomorrow?" my mom asked Sandy.

"Our bus leaves at 9:30 a.m. I think we should be there around 8:45 a.m."

Sandy gave me a sad look, and I grabbed her hand under the table. I think that it finally hit her that this was her last night with me. And about that time, it hit me as well.

After dinner, Sandy and I decided to go for a walk around the block. As we walked, Sandy broke the ice first.

"When will I see you again, Kyle?" she asked sadly.

"Maybe we can get together this summer," I said, trying to cheer her up.

I knew that this was not the answer that Sandy wanted to hear, but I didn't know what else to say. We continued to walk, neither one of us saying a word. *C'mon, Kyle, think,* I said to myself. I was never good at situations like this, and to be honest, I had never been in this situation before. Then Sandy said something that really tore into me.

"This is so unfair, Kyle. Just when I found you, I need to leave you again."

I saw a tear running down Sandy's face. We stopped walking, and I gave Sandy a hug. I didn't know what to say or do. At this time when Sandy needed me the most, I was unable to help her. I don't know why, but at that moment, I felt really confused about everything. We walked the rest of the way home silently.

By the time we got back to the house, everyone was getting cleaned up and ready for bed. Sandy went into the bathroom, and I took a shower downstairs. When I came back upstairs, Sandy was lying down where I slept in the upstairs family room. I sat down next to her, and she smiled at me.

"Did you expect me to sleep anywhere else?" she said, managing a smile.

I lay down next to her, and she put her head on my shoulder. Everything seemed so perfect, or so I thought. But why couldn't I let myself go? What was holding me back? Why couldn't I reciprocate unconditionally what Sandy was trying to give me? I had more questions than answers running through my brain, and this was beginning to scare me. What was I so afraid of?

Goodbye

Morning came way too fast for us. It didn't help that we overslept and had to hurry to get to the bus station. We didn't even have time to eat breakfast. As we loaded the car, my parents and Kevin came out to say goodbye to my friends.

"It was so nice meeting all of you," my mother said with a smile. "Feel free to visit us whenever you like."

"I'm going to practice and beat you, Chester," Kevin snarled at Chester.

As everyone exchanged hugs, I heard my mom say to Sandy, "Kyle is so lucky to have found you."

Sandy looked at my mom, smiled sadly, and said, "It seems as though I am always saying goodbye to him."

We loaded everything into the car and headed to the bus station. Sandy just sat there staring out the window. I didn't know what to say, which probably made the silence worse. There was actually so much that I wanted to say to her, but for whatever reason, the words wouldn't come out.

Soon we were at the bus station. The bus just arrived and would be boarding shortly. Chester and Maria both gave me a hug and went inside to check in, leaving Sandy and me alone. Sandy came up to me and gave me a hug. I could tell that something was bothering her. Then without saying a single word, she gave me a kiss, put a letter in my hand, and ran into the terminal.

I just stood there. What had just happened? I looked at the letter in my hand.

Oh my god, I thought. What did I do? I walked back to my car with the letter in my hand. I was afraid to open it for fear of what it might say. I got into my car and just sat there.

I must have sat there for ten minutes staring at the letter. Finally, I couldn't take it anymore. I ripped the letter open and proceeded to read the letter. This is what it said:

> Dear Kyle,
>
> Why is it that I always seem to be saying goodbye to you? Will we ever truly be together? Every moment that I spend with you just reinforces what I already know. You are the one for me, Kyle. I know my feelings for you are true, Kyle, but what worries me is what you are feeling inside your heart. I am not sure about your feelings toward me, and that uncertainty is killing me inside. I cannot make you love me, Kyle. If your heart points you in another direction, I will not stand in your way. Search your feelings, Kyle. Do what is right for you. I will be here waiting patiently, but I will not wait forever.
>
> I love you,
> Sandy

I couldn't believe what I was reading. I felt like such a jerk. As I drove home, I really didn't feel like going in for work. I called my dad and asked him if I could take the day off. He said that he understood and told me to stay at home.

As I got home, all I wanted was to be alone. I headed upstairs into my room. On my bed was a picture of Sandy and me at the park. I stared at the picture for a moment, and then I placed it upon my desk. Then I looked at myself in the mirror. I really didn't like what I saw. *Who am I?* I thought as I threw myself upon my bed.

Back to the Grind

After the weekend, it was so hard for me to get back into work mode. Part of me wanted to go back to school with them so badly. I really did miss the college life, and part of me felt that it was unfair for me to give it up. But in reality, it was my choice. No one twisted my arm or held a gun to my head; it was totally my decision. I did it for my family and our family business. I did what I thought was right.

It's been a week since my friends have left. I don't why, but for some reason, I feel a little depressed. Work is fine, but a part of me feels so empty. I also could not get Sandy's letter out of my mind. Why is it that I can't give my heart to the girl of my dreams? I have not tried to contact her since she left. I'm afraid of what she might say to me. Is love really this difficult? I am in a funk, and this funk is slowly bringing me down.

I needed to get my mind back on work, so I decided to do the monthly inventory a few days early. It's a tedious process, but I felt it would take my mind off Sandy. Boy, was I wrong. What would normally take me an hour per aisle was taking me half a day to do. I would count and recount almost every product on the shelf. My inventory sheet was starting to look like scratch paper. This caught the eye of my dad.

"Son, can you come to the office after you're done with that aisle?" he said, concerned.

I looked over to him and said, "Is anything wrong?"

"No, son," he replied. "I just want to go over something with you."

Oh great, I thought. *One more thing to worry about.* Just then, one of my high school buddies walked into the store.

My friend waved to me and said, "Hey, Kyle, can you help me find some bolts?"

"Sure thing, Marty," I responded. "Let me finish counting this first."

Maybe this will help clear my mind, I thought. I walked over to the nuts and bolts section and shook Marty's hand.

"What's up, Marty? What do you need?" I asked.

"I'm looking for some three-quarter-inch stainless bolts," Marty replied. "Also, I may need some stainless washers too."

I began looking through the stainless bolt section when Marty asked, "What happened to that girl Sandy? She was awesome at volleyball."

Oh, darn, I thought, *this is not going to help.*

"She went back to college," I replied, handing Marty the bolt.

"Is she your girlfriend?" Marty asked me.

I stood their silently. I really didn't know how to answer that question. Then Marty said, "If she's available, hook me up, man."

Again, I stood their silently. But inside, my mind was racing. I remembered the last words in Sandy's letter: "But I will not wait forever." And that's when I finally realized that I may lose her.

Father Knows Best

I walked into the office at the store. My dad was busy adding, trying to punch some invoices into the computer. *At least he's trying,* I thought.

"You wanted to talk to me, Dad?"

Dad looked up from the stack of papers and smiled. He took off his glasses and put them down on his messy desk. I could tell that whatever it is that he wants to talk about was pretty important.

"Getting the hang of it?" I asked my dad, trying to break the ice.

"I'm trying, son," he said smiling. "I guess you can teach an old dog new tricks."

"So what's up? Is there something wrong?"

"Well, son," my dad said stoically. "You tell me."

Oh god, I thought. *Was it that obvious?*

"What do you mean?" I asked my dad, trying to play it off.

"Well, Kyle, for one thing, you have been making a lot of mistakes with the inventory. Usually, I'm the one who makes the mistakes. Second, you've been late to work and very forgetful about things you need to do. I may not be a computer expert, but I know when something is bothering my son."

My dad could read me like a book. There was no use in hiding it anymore. I needed his wisdom right now, even if it was a bit outdated.

"Did Mom notice also?" I asked with a wry smile on my face.

My dad just laughed and said, "Son, I think the whole town knows."

"Well, Dad," I said looking down at his desk. "As you probably know, it is about a girl."

My dad nodded. I could tell that he already knew.

"Tell me something, son," my dad said in his father-knows-best tone. "As far as I can tell, Sandy loves you very much. What's holding you back?"

I sat there for a moment, thinking about what my dad just asked me. I never expected love to be so difficult. I never thought my life would be so difficult. I had put my family before me because that's what I thought was right. It was my sacrifice to save my family's business. But I never realized that this sacrifice would come with a price.

I looked up to my dad, who was looking back at me. Looking into his eyes, it was as though he understood what I was going through.

Then he spoke. "Kyle, when you decided to stay back and help me with the store, I wasn't in total agreement with it."

"Huh?" I looked at my dad is disbelief.

"Kyle, you're barely nineteen years old. You have your whole life ahead of you. I would never have asked you to do what you did. You need to forge your own path in life, and nobody can take that away from you."

And that's when I spoke. "Dad, at first, I did what I did out of concern for you and Mom. But being in the store, learning to run a business, and making that business work, it's in my blood. This is where I want to be, Dad. What I learn here not a textbook can teach me. This is what I want to do, Dad. This is my destiny."

"Is Sandy your destiny also?" my dad said, deflating my ego with one fatal swoop.

"I thought she was," I said sadly.

"You know, son," my dad jumped in. "She still can be. But it's really up to you."

I sat there thinking about what my father said. There was one problem with his theory though. I was here, and she was there.

"You know, son, there's no reason why you can't have your cake and eat it too."

Listening to my dad, I was so proud to be his son. Now all I have to do is find a way to have my cake and eat it too.

Mother Knows Best

I decided to give my dad a break and lock up the store. Besides, I had to fix all the mistakes on the inventory. By the time I got home, Dad was already in his room half asleep. My mom, on the other hand, was at the kitchen table waiting for me.

"Dad talked to you?" I said sarcastically, walking through the door.

My mom let out a smile, and then she said, "Most of it I already figured out for myself. You know, Kyle, when I asked you to stay back and help your father with the store, it wasn't supposed to be forever."

"It was my choice, Mom. It is what I want to do."

My mom's eyes started to tear up. "You're such a good boy, Kyle, but you can't continue to sacrifice your life for us."

"At first, it was a sacrifice," I said, taking my mother's hand. "But now I realize that this is where I want to be. This is the life that I want."

"You know that if you remain here, you may lose Sandy," my mom said sadly.

"Girls like her don't come around very often, Kyle."

The thought of me losing Sandy was tearing me apart. *I knew it, my parents knew it, and even Kevin probably knew it*, I thought.

Then my mom placed a little gold box on the table and pushed it toward me. I gave my mom a funny look.

"Open it," she said.

I picked up the box and opened it. It was a diamond ring.

"What is this?" I asked my mom looking at the ring.

"This is the first ring your father ever gave me," she said, playing with her hair. "We want you to have it, Kyle."

"I can't take this," I said, pushing it back toward my mother.

My mom pushed it back toward me and said, "Kyle, do the right thing. And besides, this way, it will still be in the family. And somewhere down the road, you can give it to your son."

I was at a loss for words. The diamond sparkled beautifully holding it up to the light.

"I can't thank you and Dad enough," I said to my mother.

"You already have, son," my mother replied. "Now go and fulfill your destiny."

I gave my mother a hug and went upstairs with the ring. *I need a plan*, I thought. I will call Chester in the morning.

School Day Blues

"Sandy, wake up. Sandy, you are not missing another class."

I grabbed my pillow and threw it at Maria. Since I left Kyle, I haven't felt like doing much of anything. Why did I write Kyle that stupid letter?

He probably hates me by now. I don't feel like going to class or studying. *Poor Maria*, I thought, *she's only trying to help.*

I dragged myself out of bed and headed into the bathroom. As I was brushing my teeth, I looked at myself in the mirror. Who was I? Who was I becoming? I really didn't like what I saw.

Today I had Ms. Miller's class. Ms. Miller's class is the one class that I am still doing well in. She did give me an "A" on my paper and said that it brought a tear to her eye. Although I really like Ms. Miller, I have been avoiding her lately. I just don't feel like talking to anyone about Kyle right now.

As I walked to class with Maria, it amazed me how many things make me think of Kyle. We were on campus for only a short time together, and it seemed so long ago, but the little memories that we shared seemed forever ingrained in my mind.

"You know, Sandy," Maria said, bringing me back to reality. "If you don't get your act in gear, you're going to be a freshman all your life."

I didn't even react to her. I just turned the other way. As we got to Ms. Miller's classroom, Ms. Miller was standing by the door. It was as though she was waiting for me.

I tried to rush past her, but she saw me and called my name.

"Sandy," she said, "can you meet me later today?"

"Sure, Ms. Miller," I said meekly.

I walked to my desk and put my head on the table. Maria just laughed at me.

"You knew she was going to ask you," Maria said sarcastically.

As Ms. Miller started her lecture, I started to daydream. I turned around to look out the window, and Kyle was standing there, waving to me. I got up from my chair and walked out the door. Instead of being by the window, Kyle was now up by the adjacent classrooms, still waving. The closer I got, the farther he got.

Then Maria gave me an elbow, bringing me back down to earth. I began to wonder what this dream meant. Were we destined to be apart forever? I didn't even feel like crying anymore. If I didn't hit rock bottom, I was very close to it. Here I was, nineteen and confused and afraid. I just wanted to run away.

Ms. Miller Is Human

As I walked down the hall to Ms. Miller's office, I had a tremendous sense of déjà vu come over me. Last time I was here, Ms. Miller told me to go to Kyle, which I did. Looking back, I found myself questioning whether that was really the right thing to do. I was confused before I went to Kyle, and now it seemed that my confusion has gotten worse. I know that Ms. Miller was only trying to help, and in the end, it was my decision to do it.

I walked into Ms. Miller's office without knocking. It seems that she already knew that I was here.

"Hello, Sandy," Ms. Miller said, smiling. "I'm so glad you came."

"Why did you call me in?" I responded forcing myself to smile.

Ms. Miller got up from her desk and walked around her office, looking at her many posters.

"Well, Sandy," she said staring at Kyle's poster. "How did it go?"

I sat there thinking about what to say to her. I decided to go with the truth. I turned to Ms. Miller, and then I told my story to her.

I told her about how we surprised Kyle at the store and that his initial reaction was not what I expected. I then told her about Kyle's parents and how nice they were to me. Through it all, Ms. Miller just sat there and nodded at me without saying a word.

Then I told Ms. Miller how Kyle was beginning to open up to me as time went on, about how we held hands and our first kiss. This brought a smile to Ms. Miller's face.

But then I told her how Kyle began wavering again and how confused he was with the whole thing. I told her how I left him but giving him a letter and running off.

"What did the letter say?" Ms. Miller asked solemnly.

"I told him that I would wait patiently for him but that I would not wait forever."

"Oh, Sandy," Ms. Miller said sadly, "maybe it wasn't meant to be. You can't force love to happen."

"Have you ever been in love, Ms. Miller?" I asked, catching her by surprise with this question.

Ms. Miller sat there in a daze. I could tell that she felt bad for telling me to go see Kyle.

"Sandy, what I am about to tell you must never leave this room."

I nodded at Ms. Miller and told her I promise.

"When I first got a job as a teacher a long time ago, I did fall in love. The only problem was I fell in love with a student of mine."

I looked at Ms. Miller in shock and amazement.

"He was my student aide at my first teaching job," Ms. Miller continued on. "He would help me grade papers, and we would spend a lot of time after classes talking about life. As time went by, I found myself falling for him. At first, he didn't realize my feelings for him, but then one day out of nowhere, I told him that I loved him."

"So what happened?" I asked Ms. Miller, forgetting about my problems.

"Well," Ms. Miller said staring at the ceiling. "He fell in love with me also. He was very close to graduation, and he asked me to go with him back to his hometown of Boston after he was done with school. The problem was I had already been offered this teaching job. When it was time for him to leave, he begged me to go with him. I wanted to, but in the end, I decided to come here."

Tears were streaming from Ms. Miller's eyes. *Oh my god*, I thought, *Ms. Miller is human.*

"To make a long story short," Ms. Miller continued. "We went our separate ways and decided to break it off. For a very long time after that, there wasn't a day that went by that I wondered if I had made the right decision. Do you know, Sandy, how hard it is to live life wondering what if? I was very depressed for a long, long time. Only with the help of a few excellent drugs and a psychiatrist did I finally get over it."

I just sat there in awe of what Ms. Miller was telling me.

Then Ms. Miller said to me, "Sandy, I didn't want you to go through your life wondering what if. That is why I told you to go to him. I am so sorry that it didn't work out for you."

I got up, walked around the desk to Ms. Miller, and gave her a hug. *How ironic*, I thought, *how similar our stories were.*

I looked at Ms. Miller and smiled. She smiled back.

"Remember," she said, looking me in the eye, "remember our pact."

I nodded and walked out of Ms. Miller's office. It wasn't the end of the world for Ms. Miller, and maybe it's not the end of the world for me. Suddenly, I didn't feel so lost. But I still did miss Kyle a lot.

Back at the Dorm

As I entered my dorm room, Maria was busy reading at her desk. I didn't say a word to her, but before I could hit my bed, Maria fired the first shot.

"So?" Maria turned and said to me impatiently.

"So what?" I replied sarcastically.

"You know what," Maria said angrily.

"I promised not to tell," I said to Maria, pretending to turn a lock on my lips and throwing the key away.

"You're no fun," Maria said, turning back to her textbook.

I did tell Maria that Ms. Miller was once in love and that she is human after all. *A promise is a promise*, I told myself even though I really did want to tell Maria everything.

Just then, Chester walked into the room. Before Chester could say anything, Maria said out loud, "Don't bother asking, she won't tell."

"What do you mean?" Chester said sarcastically. "I just wanted to see if you guys wanted to go eat dinner."

Maria just rolled her eyes and continued to read. I just looked at Chester and smiled.

"I'll go with you, Chester," I said, which, I could tell, really made him happy.

Maria threw her book on the bed and said, "Fine, you guys win."

"Maria, you don't have to go," Chester said, obviously trying to get a rise out of Maria.

I just sat there and laughed. I haven't had much to laugh about recently, and to be honest, it felt really good.

"Where are we eating?" I asked.

Chester looked at Maria, smiled, and said, "I hear there's a new waiter working at the pizza parlor, and he's supposed to be really hot."

Maria just sat there rolling her eyes. I think that, this time, she was really mad at Chester. Chester and Maria were not the perfect couple by far, but I admired how they manage to keep it going.

"Pizza sounds good," I said to Chester.

The pizza parlor did bring back memories of Kyle; it's where we kind of broke the ice. I wondered if being there tonight will make me sad again. I wondered if I would ever see Kyle again.

Chester went back upstairs to grab his wallet, while Maria and I got ready for dinner.

"You are so lucky," I said to Maria.

Maria turned to me and said, "I guess so, even if he can be a pain in the ass sometimes."

"It's just a guy thing," I said to Maria, causing her to giggle.

Chester came back to our room wallet in hand, and we were ready to go. As we walked through campus, I began to wonder what Kyle was doing. I really started to miss him again. *All I want is one more chance*, I said to myself, staring at the stars above.

The Pizza Parlor

The pizza parlor was pretty busy for a school night. After a ten-minute wait, we were able to finally get a table. As we sat down, Chester said that he had to go to the bathroom. I sat there looking at all the students in the restaurant. It seemed like just yesterday when I surprised Kyle by taking his order.

Then Chester returned. "Did you wash your hands?" Maria asked him sarcastically.

Chester just sat there and smiled at Maria. Of course, this irritated the heck out of her. Then the waiter came to bring us water. He had a hoodie on, and I could tell that he was new at this. He came, dropped the waters, and left without saying a word.

"How rude," Maria said, a little perturbed.

"He's new," Chester said. "Give the guy a break."

"What waiter wears a hoodie?" Maria said, visibly getting upset at Chester.

"Maybe he's shy," I said, trying to deflect some of Maria's anger away from Chester.

Then the hooded waiter returned. He stood behind me with his order pad covering his face.

"What can I get for you fine people?" the waiter said.

"Why don't you order, Sandy?" Chester said smiling.

"You guys trust me?" I replied.

"Whatever you want, Sandy. Remember, my treat."

I turned to the waiter and said, "How about a large combo pizza and a pitcher of iced tea."

The waiter wrote down the order and left without saying another word. Maria was really starting to get upset at the unprofessionalism of the new waiter.

"Jeez, you think they'd train these guys?" she said angrily.

Sometimes I feel sorry for poor Chester. Maria can be bitchy at times, and she is rather high maintenance the other times.

Then the waiter returned with our pizza. He still had his hoodie on, and he pretty much dropped the pizza on our table and quickly went away.

"Talk about no class," Maria said, really pissed by now. "And what the hell is that thing in the center of the pizza?"

I quickly glanced at the object. It looked like a little box. Maria picked it up and started to look at it.

"Hey, Sandy," she said now looking confused. "It has your name on it."

Maria passed me the box, and just like she said, it had my name on it. I looked at Chester who just shrugged his shoulders at me.

"What's in it?" he said curiously.

I looked at Maria.

"Open it," she barked back at me.

I opened the box; it was a bit dark and hard to see.

"Well?" the two of them said in unison.

"I think it's another box," I said back to them.

I took out the other box and opened it. As soon as I saw what was in it, I dropped it on the table.

"What is it?" Maria said frantically.

I picked up the box, looked at it again, and passed it to Maria.

"Oh my god!" Maria screamed. "Why is there a ring on our pizza?"

I took the ring back from Maria and took it out of the box. The diamond on the ring sparkled brightly despite the limited light from the restaurant.

Just then, someone put their hand on my shoulders. I looked at Maria who looked as though she just saw a ghost.

I turned around to see who it was. This time, the person did not have the hoodie on. When I saw who it was, I nearly fainted. It was Kyle.

"Have you signed up for ObamaCare?" Kyle said smiling.

For once, my prayers have been answered.

Confusion

Kyle took off that ugly hoodie, threw away his apron, and joined us at the table. He told us how he had this all planned with the help of Chester.

"So what if I didn't agree to eat pizza?" I asked Kyle in a sassy tone.

"We would have had to go plan B," Kyle said laughing.

"What was plan B?" I asked.

"I don't know," Kyle said, looking at Chester.

Then Chester said, "Failure was not an option."

We all sat there laughing. I was laughing so hard that I forgot about the ring. I picked up the box and opened it. Then for some reason, I stopped laughing. I took the ring out of the box and put in on my finger. It was a little big, but it looked so beautiful on my finger. Everyone else stopped laughing, and soon they were all looking at the ring on my finger.

"That is for you," Kyle said softly. "I want everyone to know that you belong to me."

I looked at the ring on my finger, and then I looked at Kyle.

"Do you like it?" Kyle asked, looking a little confused.

"It's the most beautiful thing that I have ever seen," I said staring at the ring.

"And for your information, the answer is yes."

Kyle gave me a strange look and said, "Yes, you like it?"

I gave Kyle back the exact same look and said to him, "Yes, Kyle, I will marry you."

At that moment, Kyle's eyes got very big. Although I said that I would marry him as a joke, I was curious to see how Kyle would respond to this. I caught Kyle looking at Chester and shrugging his shoulders. For the first time, Chester was speechless. I was getting such a kick out of this that I decided to go one step further.

"Kyle, I want to get married right away," I said to him holding the ring up to his face. "I am going to drop out of school and go back with you to the hardware store. I can't wait to tell my mom."

Suddenly, Kyle looked very pale. He picked up his glass of water, but his hand was shaking so much that the water was spilling all over his face. *Poor Kyle*, I thought, *maybe I should stop now.*

Kyle got up, excused himself from the table, and headed to the bathroom. As soon as he was gone, I started to laugh.

"He knows that I am joking, right?" I asked Maria and Chester.

"Oh my god," Chester shrieked. "I thought you were serious. I think that Kyle probably thought that you were serious also."

"You better tell him the truth," Maria said sarcastically. "Before you give him a heart attack."

I could see Kyle making his way back from the bathroom. In a way, I felt bad for doing that to him, but it was so much fun.

As he came back to the table, I grabbed his hand and said, "Kyle, I have something to tell you."

Kyle gave me a strange look and said, "Wait, there is something that I need to do."

Kyle took the ring from me and got up from the table. Then he went down on one knee in front of me.

"Sandy," he said softly, "I never want to lose you. I want you to be in my life forever. Will you marry me?"

He put the ring on my finger. I just sat there staring at it, wondering if maybe he was trying to get me back. I looked back into his eyes, and at once, I could tell that Kyle was very serious about this. Now I started to feel really nervous. But then I started to question myself. *What am I thinking?* I said to myself. This is what I want. This is what I always wanted.

I took Kyle's hand into my own and looked into his eyes.

"Is this what you want?" I said to Kyle with a tear running down my eye.

Kyle looked at me and said, "Yes, Sandy, I've never wanted anything else more than I want this."

"Then my answer is yes."

I hadn't realized that the whole pizza parlor had gathered around us, and when I said yes, they let out a loud roar.

We both stood up and embraced. People began to tap on their glasses.

"Kiss the girl," Chester said, pumping his fist into the air.

Then we kissed. It was as though everyone in the restaurant had disappeared, and Kyle and I were alone. Everyone started to cheer more. I couldn't believe what just happened.

Reality

I spent the night with Kyle at his hotel room. The adrenalin that I felt the night before has given way to reality. *Did last night really happen?* I wondered. Then I looked at the ring on my finger. It was a little big for me, but I wore it all night. Kyle would be going back home later today, and I decided to take the day off and spend it with him.

Kyle came out from the bathroom and gave me a kiss.

"You know," he said to me softly, "you can come home with me."

I really wanted to go with Kyle, but I was not sure if it was appropriate. After all, neither of us had told our parents. Never in a thousand years did I expect myself to be engaged at nineteen, and I'm sure that Kyle felt the same way. Somehow we needed to break the news to our parents in a somewhat dignified fashion.

"Kyle," I said, holding his hand, "you know as well as I do that we need to tell our parents of our engagement."

"I know," Kyle answered. "The sooner we do it, the sooner we can be together. You just need to drop out of school and come and live with me."

Kyle made it sound so easy, but whether our parents agree is the million-dollar question. My sister did not go to college, and she has done really well for herself. *That should help*, I thought, but whether my mom would approve of me getting married at such a young age was a whole other story.

"What do you think your parents are going to say about this?" I asked Kyle nervously.

Kyle got up and walked toward the hotel window.

"I don't know, Sandy," he replied. "They were the ones who told me to come here, and they were the ones who gave me the ring. I hope that they don't throw me out of the house."

"You know that they won't, Kyle," I said laughing. "Your parents love you. I just hope they feel the same way about me."

After a bit more discussion, we would both tell our parents tomorrow night. We owe it to our parents to be open and honest about this.

"Hey," Kyle said, making me jump. "You know that we could go and get married in Vegas."

I looked at Kyle and rolled my eyes.

"We can't even gamble or drink," I said to him sarcastically.

As we spent our final hour together, it occurred to me that the hardest part was probably yet to come. If either of our parents disapproved, it could really put a wrench into our plans.

"Are you nervous?" I asked Kyle quietly.

"I am," he said, turning to me. "But there is one thing that I do know. Whether it happens now or later, I will wait for you and only you."

Kyle's words made my heart swell. Hearing those words made me feel a bit more confident. But deep inside, I was still very worried.

My Mom

I woke up to the familiar sound of Maria's alarm. I looked at my finger. The brilliant diamond was staring back at me. I told Maria last night about our plans to tell our parents. I also told her that I may be dropping out of school. She didn't have much to say to me about it, but part of me believes that she really doesn't approve. *Oh well*, I thought, *she probably isn't going to be the only one to disapprove.*

I dragged myself out of bed and got ready for class. My plan was to call my mom after my last class later this afternoon. I thought about calling my sister and telling her the news first, but I decided not to. My mom should be the first to know. I owe that much to her for all that she has done for me.

"Are you ready to go?" Maria shouted.

"I am," I replied sarcastically.

We headed downstairs, where Chester was already waiting for us.

"And what are you smirking about?" Maria snarled at Chester.

"Dang," Chester said quietly to me. "What did you do to her?"

I just laughed, and we headed toward the classrooms. As we walked, I began to wonder about the possibility of leaving school. I began to question whether it was such a good idea. *Oh great*, I thought, *now my conscience shows up.*

Before I knew it, my last class had just ended. Rather than returning back to the dorm, I decided to walk around upper campus for a while and think things over. Then it hit me. What am I doing? I grabbed my phone and dialed my mom's number.

"Hi, Sandy," my mom answered happily. "I hope that nothing is wrong."

"No, Mom," I replied. "Everything is good."

"Sandy," my mother said sarcastically, "I know you better than you know yourself. Is there something on your mind?"

My mom could read me like a book. I decided to not candy coat it any longer.

"Mom, I have something to tell you. Are you sitting down?"

There was a moment of silence, and then out of nowhere, my mom said, "Sandy, are you pregnant?"

I started to laugh, "No, Mom, I am not pregnant."

My mom let out a loud sigh over the phone. *I hope my mom wouldn't have another stroke*, I thought.

"Mom," I said nervously, "Kyle asked me to marry him."

There was another moment of silence on the phone. This silence was much longer than the last one.

"What did you say?" my mom finally said.

"I said yes, Mother. It would mean everything to me if you would give us your blessing."

"Oh, Sandy," my mother replied, her voice starting to crack. "Of course, you have my blessing.

"I love you, Mom," I said, breaking out in tears.

"I love you too, Sandy," my mom replied. "What about college?"

"Well, Mom," I said, wondering how she would take this. "Kyle wants me to go and live with him. And to tell you the truth, Mom, I really don't want to be away from him any longer."

"You know, Sandy," my mom replied. "When your sister decided to not go to college, I wasn't very happy about it. But looking at how she turned out and how successful she is now, who am I to say what is right or wrong for you? Is he still the one, Sandy?"

"Yes, Mom," I said, smiling, "he is the only one."

Having my mom's blessing meant all the world to me. As I walked back to the dorm, I had a big smile on my face, but I didn't care. I had done my part, and for the most part, it was quite harmless. Now it was all up to Kyle.

Parents

I got back home late last night. Both of my parents were already asleep, and so was Kevin. I was exhausted from the long bus ride and was really looking forward to lying in my bed again. I took a quick shower and threw myself on the bed. Before I knew it, I was asleep.

I woke up to the familiar sound of Kevin looking for his backpack and the pleasant aroma of mom's cooking. I got out of bed and headed downstairs. To my surprise, my father was still home. I was hoping to break the news to my mother first, but it looks as though I will have to break it to both of them. *This should be very interesting*, I thought as I sat down at the dining room table.

"Hey, Dad," I said, trying to break the ice, "was the store busy yesterday?"

My dad put down his paper and replied, "We did okay, but we probably weren't as busy as you were yesterday."

"So how did it go?" my mother asked, not wanting to be left out.

Oh great, I thought. It used to be so much easier when my parents pretended to not care so much about anything I did.

"Well," I said looking at my mother. "Perhaps you should have a seat."

My mother had a confused look on her face and came and sat down at the table. Then she looked at my dad.

"Oh, Kyle," she said, "don't tell me that Sandy is pregnant."

I looked at my mom and then at my dad. I could see genuine concern in their eyes. I couldn't take it anymore and burst into laughter.

"What's so funny, mister?" my mom said sarcastically.

"You guys are funny," I replied, trying to stop laughing.

"So what happened?" my mom asked, getting irritated.

I managed to compose myself, and I figured I might as well give them the short version.

"Well," I said, still trying to keep a straight face. "Sandy and I are not going to have a baby anytime soon. But I think that we might be engaged."

I wondered if there might have been a better way to break the news to them. *Well, the cat is out of the bag*, I thought. The ball was in their court. Both of my parents sat there silently. *Okay*, I thought, *they are going to let me have it now*.

Through all this, my father just sat there, his eyes moving back and forth between myself and my mom. His silence was killing me more than my mom's. He casually put down his paper and took a sip of coffee. Then he spoke.

"Kyle," he said sternly. "Is Sandy still the one?"

"Yes, Dad," I replied. "Sandy is the only one."

My dad looked at my mom, who for some reason had started crying.

"If that's the case," my dad said, taking my mom's hand. "Congratulations, Kyle."

My mom got up and came over to me and gave me a big hug.

"Oh, Kyle," she whispered, "I'm so happy for you."

As I sat there, I wondered what had just happened. It seems that this was too easy. I began to wonder how Sandy did with her mom. We had promised to talk after her last class, but the suspense was killing me. I decided to head to the hardware store and put a new display for batteries. By staying busy, I hope that the day goes by faster. I took out a picture that I had of Sandy in my wallet.

"I love you," I said, kissing the picture.

To Be or Not to Be?

The day did not go by as fast as I thought it would. Not only did I finish that battery display but I also managed to put together a lawn mower, clean the store windows, and mop all the floors.

My dad came up to me and said, "You know, son, the suspense is already killing me. I can't imagine what it's doing to you."

Dad was right. I looked at my watch. Sandy would be done with her last class in about fifteen minutes. I looked around for something else to do. My dad just shook his head and laughed. I began to tinker with the screwdriver display when my phone began to ring.

I looked at my dad, who was already looking at me. Then I looked at my phone. It was Sandy.

"Hey, you," I said surprised. "Aren't you still supposed to be in class?"

"Don't be mad at me," Sandy said giggling. "I didn't go to my last class. I couldn't take it anymore."

"Good news?" I asked grimly.

"Well," Sandy said. "That depends on your definition of good news. Do you have good news for me?"

"I do, Sandy," I said excitedly.

"Really?" Sandy said anxiously.

"Yes. As of today, I am the exclusive dealer for Foreverlast batteries."

There was a moment of silence.

"Oh," Sandy said sarcastically. "I am sooooo happy for you."

"One more thing," I said, trying hard to hold my emotions back. "My parents want to know what kind of wedding cake you want for your wedding."

"Oh," Sandy said in a slightly brighter tone. "Then I definitely have some good news for you. Can you pick me up from the bus terminal tomorrow evening?"

It seems that once Sandy got the blessing of her mother, she was so confident that my parents would approve that she already made her bus reservation for tomorrow. Not only that but she also withdrew from school and sold back all of her books at the bookstore.

I just stood there speechless. What once seemed so impossible was finally becoming a reality. My dad couldn't take it anymore also. He came over to me with his palms in the air and said, "Well?"

I gave him the thumbs-up sign, and he got out his phone and called my mom.

"Are you okay?" Sandy asked, wondering why I wasn't saying anything.

"Oh yes," I said, finally being able to speak. "We will never be apart again."

"Never," Sandy replied joyously. "Now that I found it, I will never let it go."

"Did you tell Chester and Maria?"

"Not yet," Sandy said sadly, "I will do it tonight."

I began to think about Chester and the impact that he had on Sandy and I being together. I really did miss him.

"Tell Chester that I said hi and that he should come visit me this summer."

"I will, Kyle. You know that I love you, right?"

"I love you, Sandy. I will never let you go. See you tomorrow."

Goodbye, My Friends

By the time Maria came back to the room from her last class, I was almost finished packing. I had not told Maria of my plans, but as soon as she walked in, she already knew.

"Going someplace?" Maria said sarcastically.

I walked over to Maria and gave her a hug. Maria didn't hug me back at first, but once she did, she didn't want to let go.

"What am I going to do without you?" Maria said sadly.

"You've got Chester," I said, causing her to roll her eyes. "I know that you love him, so don't act."

As if on cue, Chester entered the room. He looked at Maria who had tears running down her face, and then he looked at my packed suitcases.

"Maria," Chester said, "I told you if you didn't leave Sandy alone, she would leave you."

Maria was not amused by Chester's remark and slapped him on his shoulder. Then Chester came over to me and gave me a big hug.

"I am so happy for you, Sandy," Chester whispered into my ear. "Kyle is the luckiest guy on earth."

"Let's go out for dinner one last time," I said to both of them. "This time, it is my treat."

There was one more person that I wanted to invite to dinner, and that was Ms. Miller. It was already late in the afternoon, and I wondered if Ms. Miller was still around the campus. I looked up her number in the campus registry, and I dialed her number. The phone rang around four times, and just when I was about ready to hang up, someone answered.

"Hello," the voice said.

"Um, hello," I replied, "I'm trying to get in touch with Ms. Amanda Miller."

"Oh," the voice responded, "you're talking to her."

"Hi, Ms. Miller," I said. "This is Sandy."

"Oh, hi, Sandy. Is there something wrong?"

"No, not at all, Ms. Miller. I would like to take you to dinner tonight if you're free."

"What's the occasion?" Ms. Miller asked in a surprised tone.

"I'm leaving school tomorrow, Ms. Miller," I said sadly.

"Is there something wrong with your mother again, Sandy?"

"Not at all," I said. "I have decided to go to my true love."

"Are you going to Kyle?" Ms. Miller asked excitedly.

"Yes," I said shyly. "I am going to be with Kyle."

"Oh, Sandy," Ms. Miller said, almost yelling, "I am so happy for you. Of course, I will join you for dinner tonight. I wouldn't miss it for the world."

I told Ms. Miller to meet us at the campus center in about forty-five minutes. Ms. Miller was very instrumental in bringing me and Kyle together. There was also something that I wanted to ask her.

I decided to get washed up before dinner. Although I was so happy to finally be with Kyle, part of me was really sad to be leaving college and my friends.

Farewell Dinner

As I walked up to the campus center for my last dinner here on campus, I could not help but wonder if I would ever see this campus again. Chester and Maria were also extremely quiet. I could tell that they were taking this pretty hard.

We decided to eat at the pizza parlor. I thought that it was only fitting to have my last supper here. I have so many memories of Kyle in this place, and I was a little sad to be leaving it all behind. Just then, I heard a familiar voice calling out to me.

"Sandy," I heard the voice calling to me. "Over here."

It was Ms. Miller. I walked over to her and gave her a hug. I don't know how she does it, but she still smells so good.

"I'm so glad you're here," I said with a big smile.

"I wouldn't miss this for the world," Ms. Miller responded.

As we headed to our table, Chester's eyes were glued on Ms. Miller. Maria also noticed and said, "Ahem, you can stop drooling now."

Ms. Miller and I just laughed while Chester blushed. We proceeded to order our dinner, and I thought this was a good time to ask Ms. Miller a favor.

"Ms. Miller?" I asked shyly.

"Call me, Amanda," Ms. Miller said. "You are no longer a student here. Now you are my friend."

"Can I ask you something?" I said, wondering what she will say.

"What is it, Sandy?"

"I want you to be on my wedding party. You were so instrumental in bringing me and Kyle together that it would mean a lot to us if you would be there."

I could tell that Ms. Miller was really moved by this question. She kind of looked away for a moment, and I began to wonder if maybe she wasn't comfortable with my question.

"Sandy," Ms. Miller finally answered. "I would be honored to be on your wedding party. Do you have a date set?"

"Not yet," I replied. "I will let you know as soon as we set one."

Then I turned to Chester and Maria and said, "You know that Kyle and I are expecting both of you to be there also, right?"

"I wouldn't miss it for the world," Maria said proudly.

"Road trip!" Chester yelled out as only Chester can.

As we were eating dinner, it finally hit me that at this time tomorrow I would be with Kyle. Just the thought of that was making me so excited.

After dinner was over, I gave Ms. Miller—I mean, Amanda a great big hug and told her that I would be in touch. Chester tried to get a hug also, but Maria quickly pushed him away.

"You take care of yourself," Ms. Miller said, holding my hands.

"I will," I said, fighting back the tears in my eyes.

"And say hi to Kyle for me also," Ms. Miller said. "He is so lucky to have found someone like you. I am extremely envious of both of you."

As we left the restaurant and headed back to the dorm, now it was my turn to be quiet. Chester and Maria were arguing as to why he needed a hug from Ms. Miller.

I will miss my friends, I thought.

Morning of Truth

I really didn't sleep well last night. I must have gotten up to look at the clock about a hundred times. I really began to wonder if my clock was going backward.

Finally, I was able to fall asleep, and about an hour later, my alarm woke me back up. I jumped out of bed and quickly washed myself up in the bathroom. Maria was still asleep. Her class didn't start for another two hours.

As I finished packing, I had a feeling of sadness come over me. Why was my life so filled with goodbyes? I went over to Maria and woke her up.

"Hey, Maria," I said, almost whispering. "I will be leaving soon."

"Already?" Maria answered, sitting up in her bed.

"Yes, my taxi will be here soon."

Maria put on her robe and helped me carry my things downstairs. Chester was already downstairs and looking pretty sad. I went over to him and gave him a big hug.

"I will miss you, Sandy," Chester said sadly.

"I will miss you too, Chester," I said, trying not to cry.

Just then, my taxi pulled up. This reminded me of the day I left school to take care of my mother and how I had to say goodbye to Kyle. We loaded my things into the taxi. As I turned to them, all three of us were crying.

"Group hug," I said, holding my arms out to them.

I got into the cab and said goodbye to my friends one last time. And just like that, I was gone.

When we got to the bus station, my bus was already there waiting for me. I checked in at the counter and went directly into the bus. Before the bus even left the station, I was sound asleep.

About an hour into my journey, I woke up. Staring out my bus window, I began to wonder about the meaning of life. Most nineteen-year-olds didn't usually worry about stuff like this, but for some reason, I felt like I needed an answer. What I came out with was something totally unexpected.

As I think about my short and brief life, I come to the conclusion that life really has no true meaning. It is different for everyone. I believe that life is being where you are supposed to be, being with the people you are supposed to be with, and never ever having a doubt that this is who you are supposed to be.

Not bad, I thought as I reclined back into my seat. Watching the trees go by, I realized that life doesn't come down to one moment in time. It was a culmination of all of life's adventures, good and bad. I had so much life ahead of me and so many more moments to experience.

In no time, I was sound asleep. For the first time, I realized that this is where I am supposed to be.

Reunited

"Miss, hey, miss?" I heard a strange voice say.

I woke up to find that my bus was at the station, and I was the only one left on the bus.

"Miss, this is your final stop," the kind attendant said.

I got up from my seat, grabbed my belongings, and slowly made my way off the bus. It has been a long time since I have slept that well. I don't remember anything about the trip. As I stepped down the bus, I heard a familiar voice.

"Hey, Sandy," the voice said, getting nearer.

Before I knew it, I was in the arms of the man I love. Not only was Kyle hugging me but he also was holding me up.

"How was your trip?" Kyle asked smiling.

"It was really great," I said, trying to wake myself up. "It was so great that I don't remember a thing about it."

We walked back into the station and got my bags. Everything seemed so surreal. *Am I really here?* I began to wonder.

As we drove away from the station, I turned to Kyle. He looked back at me and took my hand.

"What are you thinking about right now?" I said to him, looking into his eyes.

This question caught Kyle off guard, I could tell. He turned away from me and continued to drive for a minute or two without saying a word. I was going to let the subject go, but then Kyle spoke.

"I'll be honest with you, Sandy," Kyle said, staring at the road in front of him. "I have been a nervous wreck."

"Why is that?" I asked. "Is there something wrong?"

"Now that you're here, not anymore," he said, looking back at me. "But prior to your arrival, I kept expecting you to call me to tell me that you had changed your mind."

"That's funny," I said giggling. "I was thinking that you were going to call me and tell me the same thing."

As we drove to Kyle's house, I think that both of us realized that this was just the beginning of our journey together. And as happy we both are to finally be with one another, there is also a lot to be afraid of. It's only natural, I guess. It's just part of human nature. But there is one thing that I know, and I believe that Kyle's knows it as well. We are both very committed to being with one another. This is the life that we chose. There is no other place that I would rather be right now and no other person that I would rather be with.

Like every other relationship, there would be good times and times when things are not so good. *One day at a time*, I thought. I closed my eyes and pinched myself. As I opened my eyes, I wanted to make sure that I wasn't dreaming.

My Life with Kyle

As we arrived at Kyle's house, I suddenly became very nervous. The last time I was here, it was only to visit. Now I am here to stay or at least I hope so. Then it hit me. I wonder where I will be sleeping tonight. I guess it isn't important.

"Welcome to the family," Kyle's mom said to me, giving me a hug.

Kyle's father also came up to me and gave me a hug. Kevin already had his baseball glove on, asking me to help him practice fielding ground balls. Only two minutes in and I already feel like part of the family.

"Kevin," Kyle's dad said, "Sandy has had a very long trip to get here. I think she must be very tired and hungry. Maybe she can practice with you another time."

"Why don't you get washed up for dinner, Sandy?" Kyle's mom said to me with a smile.

We went upstairs, and I was surprised when Kyle took my things into his room. I also noticed that he had a bigger bed in his room.

"I hope you don't mind the arrangement," Kyle said embarrassingly. "The bigger bed was my parent's idea."

I just jumped on the bed and looked at Kyle.

"Where are you sleeping?" I asked him with a mischievous smile.

I could see Kyle's face starting to turn red. He really didn't think this thing through, and it was very funny to see him squirm.

"I guess I can sleep outside," Kyle said, looking at the ground.

"Kyle, you and I are engaged. You do know what that means, right?"

"I think so," Kyle said, looking up at me.

"Then get your butt over here, and lie down next to me."

Kyle came over and lay next to me.

"Isn't this nice?" I said to Kyle, grabbing his hand.

"It's perfect," Kyle said, leaning over to try and kiss me.

Just then, Kevin came running into the room, and Kyle jumped out of bed as though he got stung by a bee.

"Mom said to come downstairs and eat," Kevin said, trying to catch his breath.

Kevin ran out of the room and headed back downstairs.

"Where were we?" I said to Kyle.

Kyle came back on the bed and looked into my eyes. There was genuineness in the way that his eyes looked at me. Seeing this in his face brought a sense of calmness over me, and at that moment, I really felt like this is where I belong.

"I love you," I said, staring back into his eyes.

"I love you, Sandy," Kyle said, coming closer to me.

And then we kissed. And it was perfect.

My New Family

I got up nice and early but not nearly early enough, I guess. Kyle already left for the store. There was once a time when saying goodbye to Kyle would make me depressed, but somehow today I felt fine, especially when I read the note that Kyle had left for me.

> Dear Sandy,
>
> As you have probably figured out, I am already at the store. You were sleeping so peacefully that I didn't have the nerve to wake you up. You're so cute when you snore.
>
> I will be back around nine thirty to bring you to the store. In the meantime, relax, go downstairs, and eat some breakfast.
>
> Love,
Kyle

I got out of bed and headed into the bathroom. As I stepped out of the room, I heard the sound of little feet scurrying down the stairs.

"She's up," I could hear Kevin telling his mom downstairs.

As I headed downstairs, I could smell the bacon, fresh brewed coffee, all the stuff that I couldn't get in school.

"Good morning, Sandy," Kyle's mom said, motioning for me to sit down.

Before I could even sit on my seat, I had a big plate of bacon, eggs, and toast in front of me at the table. I began to wonder how Kyle and all of his family looked so fit.

Kevin was at the table, writing stuff in a notebook.

"What are you writing?" I asked Kevin.

"Mom says that I have to practice my math," Kevin said, looking disinterested.

Today was a teacher's workday, so Kevin didn't have to go to school, I found out from his mother.

"I'll make a deal with you, Kevin," I said to him, drawing his interest.

"What kind of deal?"

"Well, if you do all your work, I'll play catch with you later today. Do you think that's a good deal?"

Kevin's eye's got big, and he shouted yes, pumping his fists into the air.

It's a win-win for both of us, I thought. It motivated Kevin to do his work. And it would get me some exercise, especially with all this food I'm eating.

"What are your plans for today?" Kyle's mom asked me before taking a sip of coffee.

"Kyle's coming home around nine thirty to take me back to the store," I replied before putting a piece of bacon into my mouth.

"Oh, can I go to, Mommy?" Kevin said, waving his pencil in the air.

"You have to ask your brother," his mother replied.

I must have been hungry because before I knew it, my plate was empty.

"Do you want more, Sandy?"

"No, thank you," I said, taking my dishes to the sink. "If I eat anymore, Kyle may not recognize me when he gets home."

As I washed my dishes, Kyle's mom came beside me.

"I'm so glad that Kyle found you," she whispered into my ear.

It really made me feel good to hear that from her. I made me feel as though I belong here not just for Kyle but also for everyone in my new family. I couldn't wait for Kyle to come and get me. I missed my true love.

My First Job?

It was already 9:35 a.m. Where was he?

"Kevin," I said, making his eyes grow large. "Is your brother always late?"

"Yeah, Kyle always makes me wait for him."

Just then, I heard the familiar sound of Kyle's car pulling into the driveway. *He's only ten minutes late*, I thought to myself, *I'll give him a pass on this one.*

As he entered the door, Kevin quickly shouted out, "Why do you have to be late all the time, Kyle?"

I guess that Kevin wasn't going to give him a pass.

"Is somebody being impatient?" Kyle asked Kevin, staring at me at the same time.

"Yeah, Sandy kinda is," Kevin said, throwing me under the bus.

Kyle came over to me and gave me a kiss, much to Kevin's chagrin.

"Are you ready to go?" Kyle asked me while grabbing a piece of bacon.

"I'm ready," I said, pointing to Kevin who was pouting disappointedly.

"You wanna come too, squirt?" Kyle said, making Kevin's eyes large again.

Kevin didn't even bother to answer; he quickly grabbed his coat and ran out of the house. Kyle and I walked hand in hand right behind him.

As we arrived to the store, Kevin quickly jumped out of the car and ran into the store. As I entered the store, Kyle's dad came over and gave me a hug.

"Sandy, I have a proposition for you," he said to me, causing me to wonder.

"Oh," I said with a surprised look, "what kind of proposition?"

"Well," he said, looking at Kyle, "we want to make you a job offer."

This caught me a bit off guard. I hadn't really thought about what I was going to do for work. I figured that I could always get a job waitressing, but it's not something that I had my heart set on doing.

"What do you want me to do?" I asked, looking at Kyle and then at his dad.

"Nothing in particular," Kyle's dad answered.

"Just a little bit of everything," Kyle chimed in.

I had never worked retail before, but I figured why not. It also meant that I get to spend more time with Kyle.

"I'll take it," I said, "Where do I sign?"

"Kyle, why don't you give Sandy the grand tour of the store, while Rob and I take down that old lawn mower display."

Kyle came over to me and took my hand. Then he led me to the back storeroom. Kevin was already back there, drinking a soda pop and eating cookies.

"I was going to tell you," Kyle said to me. "It was my dad's idea."

"You're lucky to have a father like him, Kyle. I barely knew my father."

As he showed me around the store, I could see the pride that Kyle had in his family's business. I could see the passion in his eyes and hear the passion in his voice. His father had taught him well.

Just one more reason to love him, I thought.

The Call

"Hey, Sandy, wake up. Sandy, are you awake?"

I slowly rolled over in my bed to see who was rude enough to wake me up. Of course, it was my man.

"Sandy," Kyle was almost pleading by now. "If you want to go in early with me, I think you should get up about now."

I got out of bed and stumbled into the bathroom. *Maybe work wasn't so much fun after all*, I thought. Just then, Kyle popped his head into the bathroom.

"Here," he said. "You need to wear this."

Kyle tossed me one of the hardware store's official shirts.

"Sorry about the color," Kyle said. "I'll get more for you later."

Actually, I kind of liked the color, sort of a cross between olive green and forest green.

"How does this look?" I asked Kyle, walking out with my new shirt on.

All Kyle could do was laugh.

"Fine," I said. "Go ahead, and be that way."

I walked back into the bedroom, where Kyle was putting on his socks.

"By the way, Kyle," I said curiously. "How much will I be making?"

Kyle started to laugh again, and then he said, "How much do you think you're worth?"

I went over to Kyle, put my arms around his head, and said, "How much do you think I'm worth?"

Kyle gave me a kiss and said, "Babe, to me, you are priceless."

We headed downstairs to eat a quick breakfast. As usual, Kyle's mom had prepared a feast fit for royalty—bacon, eggs, hotcakes, crepes with fresh fruit. I wondered how she had the time to make everything.

"Are you ready for your first day of work?" Kyle's mom asked me.

"I hope my new boss isn't so hard on me," I replied, looking at Kyle.

"I'm sure you'll do fine, Sandy. When we first opened the store, I used to go and help every day. Times were tough back then, but somehow we managed to keep the store going all these years."

I really liked Kyle's mom. She reminded me so much of my mom. She was just a ball of energy that could light up any room. I could tell that she was also a very passionate woman. No wonder Kyle turned out the way he did.

"Don't worry, Mom," Kyle said smiling. "I can always fire her if she starts messing up."

I was just about to punch Kyle in the arm when my cell phone started to ring.

I looked at the caller ID, and my heart just sank. It was my sister, Audrey. I knew right away that something was wrong.

Life's Curves

I excused myself from the table and went outside. I could tell that Kyle and his mom were really concerned, but I thought it would be best if I spoke to my sister in private.

"Hey, Audrey, how are you?"

"I'm fine," Audrey said, her voice visibly erratic. "It's Mom. She had another stroke last night."

My heart just sank. My mother was doing so well, changing her diet, making changes to her lifestyle, and really watching out for her health.

"How bad was it?" I asked, expecting to hear the worst.

"It was pretty bad, Sandy. She'll pull through, but she just can't be left alone anymore."

I was in tears hearing my sister tell me about my poor mother. She apparently suffered the stroke and fell to the ground, hitting her head on the floor. Luckily, she was able to get to the phone and call Audrey. If it was a major stroke, she could very easily have died without anyone there to help her.

"Sandy," Audrey said softly. "We can't leave her alone. It's not safe for her. I have been really busy with my business, and I don't have the time to stay with her. Is there any way that you can come back and watch her at least till she gets better?"

All that was going through my mind was this can't be happening to me. Just when Kyle and I were finally together, I would have to leave him again.

"Please, Sandy," Audrey was pleading now.

"I will try to get back home as soon as possible," I said, trying to reassure Audrey.

"Thank you, Sandy. Let me know when you're coming in, and I will pick you up."

"Hang in there, Audrey," I said, trying to make her feel better.

I got off the phone but continued to stay outside for a few minutes more. I couldn't believe how life could be so cruel. I began to worry about how Kyle was going to feel about this.

As I walked back into the house, Kyle and his mom were sitting at the dining room table staring at me. I immediately sat down and took Kyle's hand. They already knew that something was terribly wrong. I wasn't even gone, and I already began to miss my true love again.

Goodbye Again

I decided to fly back home this time. Fortunately, there was a direct flight later this afternoon, and I could be with my mom by late this evening. As I began to pack my bag, Kyle came up behind me and gave me a hug.

"Do you want me to come with you?" he said warmly.

"No," I said sadly. "I don't know how long I will have to stay with her."

I really wished that Kyle could come with me, but I could be gone for weeks, for months, maybe even a year. The thought of being away from Kyle for that long was really making me feel depressed.

I decided to call Audrey to let her know of my arrival later this evening and to get any updates on mom.

"Hey, when are coming in, Sandy?"

"I will be arriving at around 9:00 p.m. later this evening. I'll call you when I land."

"Thank you so much for doing this, Sandy," my sister said. "Mom really needs us right now."

"How is she doing?"

"She's very weak right now," Audrey said sadly. "She's been resting peacefully though, and I know she can't wait to see you."

"I will see you real soon," I said, starting to cry.

"Thank you, Sandy. I love you."

"I love you too, Audrey."

I finished my packing and called Kyle to the room.

"I'm done packing," I said to him, wiping away my tears.

"The airport is about an hour away," Kyle said, putting his arms around me. "We should leave soon."

"Kyle," I said turning toward him. "Why do you think God is doing this to us?"

I could tell that this question caught Kyle by surprise. We never really did discuss religion before, and I was interested in seeing what he would say.

"Sandy," Kyle said, looking out the window. "I think God knows that no matter what happens, we will always be together."

Kyle's answer somehow made me feel a little better about the situation. I didn't expect that answer from him, but somehow I had the feeling that, in the end, everything will be all right.

Kyle grabbed my suitcase, and we headed downstairs. Both of his parents were downstairs to see us off. I gave both of them a hug and thanked them for all of their support.

"If we can help you in anyway, Sandy, please let us know," Kyle's dad said to me.

Now I knew why Kyle is the man he is, especially when he has a role model like his dad. They were already like my family, and I found myself starting to miss them as well.

As we got to the airport, tears were running down my cheeks. I tried so hard to keep it together, but to no avail. As we embraced one last time, I wondered when I would see my Kyle again.

"I love you," I said, gazing into his eyes.

"I love you, Sandy," he replied. "I'll be here waiting for you. If you ever need me, just say the word, and I will be there."

Goodbye again; how many more times will I be saying that?

Home

As soon as I was on the plane, I was sound asleep. I was exhausted, physically and mentally. Before I knew it, the plane was landing. I called my sister to let her know that I had just touched down.

I quickly grabbed my bags and headed out the door of the baggage claim. My sister was already outside waiting for me. I walked over to her and gave her a hug. My sister and I were not really that close. She was more of a loner, while I was the girl next door. The one constant was our mom. Despite our differences, Mom always treated us very fairly.

"How's Mom?" I asked my sister as we got into her car.

"She's feeling better," my sister replied. "And I know that she can't wait to see you."

"How are you doing, Audrey?"

"I've been really busy lately. I may need to hire a few more employees. Do you need a job, Sandy?"

I just smiled. I was happy to see that Audrey's business was doing well and growing. I would be really hard for her to run her business and take care of Mom at the same time. And that's when it hit me. *I may be here for a while*, I thought. The thought of being away from Kyle was unbearable.

As we pulled into the driveway of our house, I noticed that the lights were still on. Hopefully, Mom was still up. I quickly grabbed my bags and followed Audrey into the house.

I put my bags on the floor and went straight into Mom's room. Although her eyes were closed, they opened quickly when she heard me come into the room. I could see how much of an effect this last stroke had on her. She looked very pale and very worn-down.

I sat down on the bed beside her and took her hand. She turned to me and smiled.

"Oh, Sandy," she said in a raspy voice, "I'm so happy that you are here."

"How are you feeling, Mom?" I said smiling back at her.

"I'm so tired, Sandy. That's all, I'm just really tired."

Then Audrey came into the room. "Mom has a doctor's appointment tomorrow at 10:00 a.m. I'll try to see if I can make it."

"Okay," I said. "I can take her."

Then Audrey pulled me to the side and said, "I have a long day tomorrow. I'm going to go home now."

I told Audrey to go and that I could take it from here. Mom had already fallen back asleep anyway.

I went into the kitchen to make myself a cup of coffee, and I decided to call Kyle.

"Hey," Kyle said, instantly bringing a smile to my face. "How's your mom doing?"

"She's doing better. Right now she's sleeping."

"How are you doing, Sandy?"

"I'm okay," I replied. "I really miss you, Kyle."

"I miss you too, Sandy. I missed you before you were gone."

That's my line, I thought. *No wonder I love this man.*

"I'm going to sleep now, Kyle. I'm really tired. I'll call you tomorrow."

"Okay, Sandy. Did I ever tell you how much I love you?"

"How much?" I said, smiling at the phone.

"More than you can ever imagine, my love."

"I love you, Kyle. I'll talk to you tomorrow."

I went back upstairs to check on my mom. She was sleeping soundly. I went into my room and threw myself onto the bed. Before I knew it, I was asleep.

The Doctor

I woke up nice and early, and I was really surprised to see my mother in the kitchen eating her oatmeal.

"Are you feeling better?" I asked with a smile.

"I am, dear," Mom replied. "Do we really have to go to the doctor again?"

That was just Mom being Mom. Before her stroke, everyone thought that she was indestructible. Now she is fighting for her life.

"Yes, Mother," I said sternly. "We have to go to the doctor."

I cleaned up the kitchen and started to get ready. I really hope that Audrey can be there as well. She was so busy with her cleaning business, so much so that she really doesn't have much of a social life.

I went into my mother's room to check up on her. She was sitting down, staring at herself in the mirror. I could see the fear in her eyes, and it was something that I wasn't used to seeing.

"You almost ready, Mom?"

"Yes," she said, turning to me. "We can leave soon."

The doctor's office was relatively empty. Mom went in right away. I sat nervously in the waiting room. Audrey called to say that she would be a little late but that she would definitely be there. I was relieved that Audrey would be here. Whatever happens with our mom will definitely affect both of us.

Just then, the door opened, and Audrey came walking in. I always thought that Audrey was very pretty, but lately, she has looked really worn-down. Her business and Mom's health was really taking a toll on her. *Poor Audrey*, I thought, *now who will she get support from?*

As we sat there in waiting, the silence was finally broken by a nurse walking toward us.

"Dr. Adams would like to speak with both of you now."

"Is everything okay?" Audrey asked nervously.

"It's better if you speak to him," she replied politely. "Follow me please."

We followed the nurse into the doctor's office. He was busy looking at some charts, probably our mother's chart.

"Hi," Dr. Adams said smiling. "How are both of you doing?"

"We've been better," Audrey said sarcastically. "How is our mom?"

"Your mother had another minor stroke," Dr. Adams said seriously. "That's the good news."

"And the bad news?" I asked sadly.

"The bad news is that she could have a far more severe stroke at any time. I want to start here on a low-dose aspirin regiment and see how it goes. The good news is that your mother did not suffer any loss to her motor functions. And her neurological functions all seem normal as well."

"What can we do?" we both asked in unison.

Dr. Adam's looked at his chart for a moment and then turned to both of us, removing his glasses.

"I don't think your mother should be living alone anymore. Lucky for her, this was a minor stroke. If she had suffered a major stroke, she would have died by the time help got to her. I know it's not what either of you wanted to hear, but it is what it is. Also, she could fall into severe depression, and from what I've seen with other patients, they could lose the will to fight. Because of all this, I believe that she should not be left alone for any prolonged periods."

I turned to my sister, and from the look in her eyes, I already knew what she was going to say to me. We got up and thanked the doctor and headed to the room where Mom was resting.

"You ready to go, Mom?" I asked, trying to cheer her up.

She looked at us and smiled sadly. Seeing her like this just made me want to cry.

I Knew It

As we arrived back at the house, I thought it was interesting that Audrey followed us there. I helped Mom into the house and took her to her room.

"If you need anything, please let me know. Okay, Mom?"

"I will, honey," she said quietly.

I could tell that something was bothering her, but I was too afraid to ask. She had been through a lot these past few days, and I was sure that when the time is right, she will tell me.

As I headed back to the kitchen, Audrey was there waiting for me.

"Don't you have to go back to work?" I said, grabbing a glass from the cupboard.

"I do, but before I go, we need to talk."

"Okay," I said, bracing myself for the worst.

"What are we going to do?" Audrey said, her eyes tearing up. "There is no way that I can watch Mom with my business."

I just sat there silently. I already knew what was coming.

"I will make some phone calls later today," Audrey said, wiping her eyes.

"Who are you going to call?" I asked confused.

"We are going to have to put her in a nursing home," she said sadly. "We have no choice."

This was not what I expected to hear from my sister.

"Are you crazy?" I said, definitely catching my sister by surprise.

"What other choice do we have?" she said with a frown. "Are you going to stay here and watch her?"

"I don't know," I replied. "But we can't just put her into a home. I can't do that to Mom."

Audrey got up and grabbed her bag.

"Well, you figure it out then. I'll be back later this afternoon. If you can come up with a better idea, I'll be willing to listen."

As I watched Audrey drive away, only then did it hit me. I thought that Audrey was going to ask me to stay and help her out with Mom. The only reason Audrey would put Mom in a home was because of me. I suddenly felt very bad for talking to her that way. Deep down, Audrey was only looking out for my best interest.

I walked back to the room to check on my mother. She was sound asleep. How could I put my mother into a home? The woman who sacrificed so much for me and my sister. But on the other hand, how could I stay and watch her? How long would I last being away from Kyle?

There has to be another way.

I Miss Sandy

Not having Sandy around was beginning to take its toll on me. She's been gone only two days, and already, I am having withdrawals. What if she has to stay for the whole month? Days go by longer, knowing that she's not there at the end of the day.

I took off a little early from the store today. It was slower than usual, and my dad told me to go home. As I entered the house, Mom was busy in the kitchen.

"Hey, honey," she said, trying to cheer me up. "How was work?"

"It's okay," I replied grumpily.

"No word from Sandy yet?"

"Nope," I replied.

Then like a divine intervention, my phone began to ring. It was Sandy. I ran upstairs to our room to take the call.

"Hello," Sandy said. Hearing her voice made my heart melt.

"Hey," I replied happily, "I was just thinking about you."

"Sorry I didn't get back to you sooner, Kyle. Today has been a very long day."

"That's okay, Sandy. How is everything with your mom?"

There was a pause, and I could tell that something was wrong.

"Well," Sandy said sadly, "my mom is better, but the doctor gave us some really bad news."

"What did he say?"

Sandy began to tell me what the doctor had told her, that it was not safe to leave her mother by herself and that another stroke could kill her. She also told me about Audrey's idea of putting her into a nursing home.

"I can't do it, Kyle," Sandy said, her voice cracking.

"So what are you going to do, Sandy?"

"I don't know, Kyle. I miss you so much, but for now, I am the only one who can take care of Mom."

"I miss you too, Sandy," I said, trying to cheer her up. "But you need to do what you need to do."

"I need to go, Kyle," Sandy said sadly. "My mother is calling me."

"No problem, Sandy. I love you."

"I love you too, Kyle. Can I call you later?"

"Call me anytime."

As I got off the phone, it finally hit me. There was a chance that I was not going to see Sandy for a very long time. I was upset but saddened at the same time. This was not the news that I wanted to hear, and I really missed being away from my true love.

The Dilemma

I must have fallen asleep. I was awakened by my mother calling me to come and eat dinner. As I made my way into the kitchen, everyone was suspiciously very quiet. Even Kevin didn't say a word. As I sat down at the table, that's when it all began.

"So, Kyle," my mom said, breaking the ice, "how's everything with Sandy and her mother?"

"Not too good," I said, unable to hide my disappointment.

"Where did Sandy go?" Kevin asked, scratching his head.

"She needed to go back home, son," my father said, looking away from his paper. "Sandy's mother is sick, and she needs Sandy's help."

I told my parents what Sandy had told me, how another stroke could kill her mother and that she couldn't be left alone anymore. I also told them about Sandy's sister wanting to put their mother into a home.

"Sandy just can't do it," I said, looking at my parents.

"Just tell Sandy to bring her mother over here," Kevin said out loud sarcastically.

"It's not that simple," I told Kevin. "Are you going to help take care of her?"

"I can bring her cookies and juice," Kevin said proudly.

I could tell that Kevin missed Sandy. I think that everyone missed Sandy, but no one missed her more than me.

As we ate dinner, my mom and dad were still suspiciously very quiet. I could tell that something was going through their minds. Mom made her special fried chicken, which Kevin and I ate like there was no tomorrow.

After dinner, I excused myself from the table and headed back upstairs. I decided to give Sandy a call.

"Guess who?" I said.

"Hey," Sandy said softly. "I was just taking a nap."

"Oh," I said, feeling bad. "Should I call you back?"

"Don't be silly. How is everyone back home?"

It's funny hearing Sandy call our house home, especially since she really was home.

"Everyone's doing fine," I said happily. "But I think Kevin really misses you."

Sandy started to laugh. It was nice to hear her laugh. With all that she's been going through, she still managed to stay strong.

"How's your mom?"

"She's feeling better," Sandy said sadly, "but I think that she is very depressed."

"Did Audrey talk to you about the home?"

"Audrey called me, but she was unable to find a really suitable home for Mom. Some of the places were too expensive. Others seemed kind of dreary. She is going to try to call more places tomorrow."

"I wish I was there with you," I said with a tear in my eye.

"I wish you were here too, Kyle," she said softly.

We chatted for over an hour, not about anything in particular. It was just good to hear her voice. I could tell that Sandy was tired, and I decided to let her go.

As I lay in my bed, I wondered how long Sandy was going to be away from me. I wondered if there was anything I could do to help her mother. I could tell that this was going to be a long night.

Next Day at Work

I didn't sleep well last night. The thought of Sandy being away from me for any prolonged period was really unsettling. The fact that we were actually engaged did help though. At least I knew that, eventually, Sandy would be mine someday.

As I arrived at the hardware store, I decided to start working on the quarterly inventory. I figured that doing something like this would make the day go by faster. Boy, was I wrong. At the end of the first hour, my inventory sheet was filled with a bunch of chicken scratch and scribbled numbers.

Frustrated, I went into the office, threw my papers on the desk, and threw my hands into the air. Of course, this charade caught the attention of my father.

"Bad day, son?" he asked me sarcastically.

I felt bad for disturbing my father; normally, I don't lose control like that. I gathered my papers into a neat stack, put my hands together, and smiled.

"What makes you say that?" I replied.

"Well, for one thing, you are not very good at hiding your emotions."

My dad was right; I was not playing with a full deck right now. I felt so helpless not being able to help Sandy in her time of need.

"You know, son," my dad said, looking at me. "Sometimes when things are not going well, I remember what your grandfather used to tell me."

I looked at my dad. *Oh my god*, I thought. *He is going to tell me some great words of wisdom that will make all of this go away.*

"He used to tell me, 'Son, if there ever comes a day when life is kicking you in the ass, do what I do. Grab a bottle of tequila, and drink till you pass out. Nothing will be worse than the hangover that you will experience once you regain consciousness.'"

"Ha, ha, ha," I said, giving my father a rather irritated look.

"Sorry, son," he said laughing, "It worked for me."

"Do you have a bottle of tequila?" I asked sarcastically.

He opened the bottom drawer of his desk, and wouldn't you know it, he actually had a bottle of tequila.

"I'm going to go home early today, son," my father said, changing the subject.

"Anything wrong?"

"No, I'm just going to help your mother out at home."

"Sure," I said. "I'll lock up."

My father looked at the scribble inventory on my desk and then passed me the tequila.

"You need this more than me," he said with a smile, leaving the office.

I put the bottle on my desk, looked at the inventory, and shook my head. Then I opened the bottle and took a shot. Whoa, I could get used to this.

My Sweetheart

After spending the latter part of the day fixing my inventory sheet, I decided to give Sandy a call before I locked up.

"Hey, you," Sandy said, her voice was like music to my ears.

"Hey," I replied eagerly. "Guess what?"

"Oh no," Sandy said playfully. "What did you do now?"

"Nothing bad, I think I'm going to start drinking."

I told Sandy about what my grandfather told my father to do whenever he was feeling blue. I also told her how it just so happened that my father had a bottle of tequila in his desk.

"Sounds good," Sandy said laughing. "Save some for me."

"So how's the search for a home coming along?"

"Well, Audrey did find this one place that looks really good. It has excellent reviews about the staff and all the amenities that they provide."

"Awesome," I said excitedly. "When can she move in?"

There was a moment of silence, and that's when I figured that there must be a catch.

"Well," Sandy said disappointingly, "there is one problem with the place. It's really expensive, and I don't think that we can afford it."

Talk about being on top of the world one minute and falling down the next. That tequila was really looking quite tempting right about now.

"What a bummer," I said, trying to hide my disappointment.

"I guess we are just going to have to keep looking," Sandy said sadly.

"I wish I could be of more help to you, Sandy. I feel so helpless over here."

"I wish I could be with you," Sandy replied. "Being away from you is the hardest part of all of this."

Just then, I started to feel really depressed. *This process could really take a long time*, I thought. Even though we were engaged, it was as though we were further apart than ever.

"I need to go, Kyle. Mom is calling me. Will you call me later tonight?"

"Of course, I will. I need to close up the store anyway."

"I love you, Kyle."

"I love you, Sandy. Hang in there, babe."

I started to lock up the store, wondering how long we will be apart. Sandy was running out of options, and there was nothing that I could do to help. That was the hardest part, not being there for her when she needed me the most. I grabbed the bottle of tequila and put it in my pocket. *I may need this later tonight*, I thought as I exited the store.

At Home

As I arrived home, I noticed that there were a lot of boxes out by the front door. I walked past them to find more boxes and stuff inside the house. I went into the kitchen to look for my parents, but they weren't there. I could hear them though and followed the sound of their voices. Finally, I found them in the storage room.

"What are you guys doing?" I asked, scratching my head.

Mom and Dad were packing boxes and moving stuff around, acting like I wasn't there.

"Hello," I said. "Can you hear me?"

Kevin popped his head out from a large box.

"Kyle, guess what?" he said at the top of his lungs.

"What's going on, Kevin?"

"This is going to be the room of Sandy's mom."

"What?"

"Don't just stand there, Kyle, grab a box," my mother said to me sarcastically.

"What's going on?" I asked her, grabbing the box.

"Well, this room was actually supposed to be a bedroom. But for the longest time, it's been more like a storage room."

"Where are we going to put all this stuff?" I asked, looking at my dad.

"We have tons of room in our warehouse at the store," my dad said, picking up a box.

I couldn't believe what I was hearing. No wonder my dad went home early today. I wonder when he and my mom planned all of this.

"We made this room downstairs with the idea that if your mother and I ever got too old to walk up the steps, then we could just stay down here."

"I bet you didn't know that there is even a bathroom down here," my mom said, pointing at the door.

I grabbed three boxes and carried them outside. *This could really work*, I thought. Suddenly, a strange feeling came over me. It was like a sense of gratitude that I had never felt before. After all the sacrifices that they made for me, here they were, making probably the biggest sacrifice ever and for someone that we've all never met.

After a few more hours of packing, the room was finally done.

"We just need to go pick up a dresser," my dad said, wiping the sweat from his brow. "But first, there is something that you need to do, Kyle."

I looked at my dad and said, "What is that?"

"You need to tell Sandy to come back home."

What If

At first, I was so excited about bringing Sandy and her mom home here to live with us, but as I thought about it more, I began to have some doubts. I'm sure that Sandy would have no problems coming back, but what if her mom refused? After all, she would be leaving the only home she ever knew for a strange new place. And how would Audrey feel about all of this?

I decided that there was only one way to find out. I was never one to shy away from a problem, and with that, I started to dial Sandy's number.

"Hey, you," Sandy answered happily.

"Hey, babe," I replied. "How is everything going?"

"Mom's starting to feel better, so that's a good thing. But as far as finding her a place to stay, that's search is not going very well."

This was my chance, I thought.

"Hey, Sandy, I have a proposition for you."

"Oh really, Kyle?" Sandy said curiously. "What is it?"

"My parents want you to come home. Oh yeah, and one more thing, they want you to bring your mother with you."

Sandy did not answer right away, and the long pause made me wonder if perhaps I had said something wrong.

"Are you still there?" I said.

"Yes," Sandy replied, perhaps in a bit of shock. "How would we do this?"

I began to tell Sandy about my parents cleaning up the old storage room downstairs. I told her that this room was actually a bedroom with its own bathroom.

"I don't know what to say, Kyle. I can't believe that your parents would do this for us."

"I was as shocked as you when I came home from work and found them cleaning out the room."

I knew that Sandy would be excited, but now it was time for the important question.

"Sandy," I said solemnly. "How would your mother feel about moving here? Do you think she would go for it?"

"I don't know, Kyle," Sandy replied. "As long as I know, this has always been her home."

"Why don't you ask her and let me know?"

"She's asleep right now. I will talk to her as soon as she wakes up. Please thank your parents for me. I really miss them also."

"Talk to her, and call me back later. I love you, Sandy."

"I will, Kyle. I love you too."

Now all I could do was wait.

Audrey

How much longer will my mother sleep? I couldn't wait to tell her what Kyle had told me. Arrgh! I just want to wake her up. Then I thought about it. I better call Audrey and tell her about the plan. I really hope that she will be okay with it, but deep down, I really wasn't so sure.

"Hey, Audrey," I said calmly. "How are things going?"

"Oh my god," Audrey said sarcastically. "I wish I could take a break from work and just take a vacation."

Audrey continued to tell me how busy her business had become. From new clients to businesses, she was swamped.

"I think that I may need to expand, Sandy. Hey, do you need a job?"

I just laughed and said, "Thanks, but no thanks."

"I just want to thank you for helping me with Mom. I know it's hard for you to be away from Kyle, and I really wish that I could help out more."

"Don't worry about it," I said, seeing my chance. "We may have an answer to our problems."

"Really?" Audrey said in a very curious tone.

I began to tell her what Kyle had proposed to me, how Mom and I would go to live with Kyle and his parents, and how Mom would get the care that she needs without putting a strain on Audrey.

"What do you think?" I asked.

There was a moment of silence, and I began to wonder if maybe Audrey was against this idea. Then she spoke.

"Wow," she said softly. "Kyle's family would do that for us? I don't know what you did to get this guy, Sandy, but you better not ever let him go. Does he have a brother?"

Together we laughed. It was probably the first time we laughed together in a long time.

"We won't be that far away," I said to Audrey. "It will give you a reason to take a vacation and travel."

"I am going to miss you guys," Audrey said, her voice starting to crack.

"Well, don't worry about that yet. I still need to tell the plan to Mom. What if she does not want to go?"

"Have faith," Audrey said. "Good things always happen to good people."

We said our goodbyes, and I promised Audrey that I would call her after talking to Mom. I got the blessing of one; now I need the blessing of the other.

Moment of Truth

After speaking with Audrey, I went into the kitchen to make myself a cup of tea. As I sat down drinking the tea, a sudden uneasiness came over me. Would my mother who had lived here all of her life want to move to someplace different and strange?

I got up and walked over to her room to see what she was doing. To my surprise, she was wide awake.

"Hey, why didn't you call me?" I said to her in a surprised tone.

"I don't know," my mother replied softly. "I was just thinking."

"What about?"

"About you Sandy."

Her reply caught me off guard. And I quickly asked her if everything was okay.

"No," my mother said abruptly. "Everything is not okay, at least not to me."

"What's wrong?" I asked almost in a state of panic.

My mother sat up and told me to sit down on the bed beside her. She ran her fingers through my hair and smiled.

"I'm keeping you away from your true love, Sandy. And as far as I'm concerned, that is not okay."

"Kyle and I both understand the situation," I said, taking her hand. "What if I told you there might be a way for all of us to be together?"

My mom looked at me with a puzzled look on her face. Then she said, "How?"

"Come with me to Kyle's house. They have an extra room for you, and they really want you to come and live with them."

My mother sat there speechless.

"What do you think?" I asked, wanting a response.

"What about Audrey?" my mom asked, looking down at our hands.

"Audrey is fine with it. I spoke to her about it earlier, and she wants what's best for everybody, including you."

Tears started to roll down my mother's face. I could tell that she was really touched by the generosity of Kyle's family.

"Can I have the night to think about it?" she said softly.

"Of course, you can," I said, squeezing her hand. "I know that this cannot be an easy decision for you. Take all the time that you need."

I went back to the kitchen to make my mother a bowl of soup. It was all up to her now. And that's what will make this decision such a tough one. I really felt bad for asking her to make such a difficult decision. Only time will tell.

The Real Moment of Truth

I didn't sleep well last night. I kept tossing and turning, wondering what my mother would decide. Finally, I couldn't take it anymore. I got up and walked over to her room. To my surprise, the light was on, and she was already up.

"Can't sleep?" I asked, walking into her room.

"Not too well," she replied. "I did a lot of thinking last night."

"Have you come to a decision?"

"Yes, I have," she quickly replied. "Sit down, and let me tell you what I have decided."

I pulled a chair next to the bed and sat down. My mother sat up in her bed and looked at me. *Oh my god*, I thought. *What if I don't like what she says?*

"You once told me, Sandy, that Kyle is the one. Do you still believe that to be true?"

"Yes, Mother," I replied. "Kyle is the one for me."

"If that is the case," she said, looking out the window. "I will go with you to stay at his house. But there is one condition."

"Okay," I said nervously. "What is the condition?"

"Originally, I was going to leave the house to you and Audrey. I figured that later in life, if you needed money, then you could sell the house and split it with her."

"Okay," I said again. "So what is the condition?"

"I want to give the house to Audrey. In a way, I feel like I am deserting her. It is the least that I can do to make sure that she is taken care of."

"Oh, Mother," I said, trying to cheer her up, "Audrey would never think that."

"I've kept you and Kyle apart long enough. It's time for the two of you to begin your lives together as one. I'll ask Dr. Taylor when it will be safe for me to travel."

I jumped on the bed and gave my mother a big hug, nearly knocking her over.

"Hey, Sandy," she said, managing a laugh. "I'm still a bit weak, you know."

I grabbed my phone and headed downstairs. There were two people that I needed to call, Audrey and then Kyle.

I told Audrey about Mom's answer and leaving the house to her. I also told her that she better come to visit us whenever she has the chance. I could tell that Audrey was happy for me but a little sad that Mom would be moving away. But knowing that Mom was going to be taken care of lifted a huge weight off her shoulders.

"Thank you," I said to Audrey.

"No," she quickly replied back. "Thank you, Sandy."

Now all I needed to do was tell Kyle. But I wanted to do that in a special way.

I'm Coming Home

"Hello, anyone home?" I asked.

"Depends on what your definition of home is," said the kind voice in the other end.

"Well," I said sassily. "Home is where the person I love lives."

"And when are you coming home to be with the person you love?"

"As soon as I can," I replied laughing.

"What? Really? You sure? How? What?"

"Kyle, take a deep breath," I said sarcastically. "I'm coming soon as soon as my mother is well enough to travel."

Hearing the joy in Kyle's voice made me wish I was already there. I have never felt this way about anyone else in my life, and it only reinforced what I already knew, that Kyle is the one for me.

"I better tell my parents the good news," Kyle beamed. "The room is pretty much done, and it looks awesome."

"You sure your parents are okay with this, right?"

"Remember, it was initially their idea. I think it will be good for my mother to have someone around during the day to keep her company."

There was no way that we could thank Kyle's family enough for helping me and my mother through this. Not only that, I could never thank them enough for Kyle. When I look at Kyle, I can see how much of an influence his family has had over him. Kyle was the perfect blend of gentleman, comedian, and kook. And when I say kook, I mean it in a good way.

"My mother goes back to the doctor the day after tomorrow," I said. "Hopefully, the doctor can give us some idea as to when she'll be able to travel."

"I'll keep my fingers and toes crossed," Kyle said kookily.

"I will too, sweetie," I replied in a rather kooky voice myself.

"Oh yeah, I almost forgot. Kevin got a new baseball glove, and he wants you to help him with his fielding."

"Tell Kevin he's on. Hey, I gotta get going. I'll call you tomorrow?"

"I'll be waiting," Kyle said happily.

"I love you, Kyle."

"I love you too, Sandy."

Visit to the Doctor

"Hey, Mom, are you ready to go? We are going to be late."

"I'm coming," my mom said fussily, "I only got one speed these days, and it's extra slow."

Hopefully today we can get some answers about my mom's health and her ability to travel. Audrey got away from her busy schedule and will meet us at the clinic.

I finally got my mother into the car, and we drove down toward the clinic. I began to wonder what kind of things was going through her mind.

"How are you feeling, Mom?" I asked, trying to get some answers.

"I've been better," she replied. "Maybe I should ask you how you are feeling, Sandy."

I wasn't prepared for Mom's question. I sat there silently as my mind went blank.

"I think I'm feeling all right," I said finally.

"You can't hide anything from me, Sandy. I don't think that you are feeling all right at all."

My mom could read me like a book. Of course, there was so much going through my mind, my mom's health, Audrey, and Kyle.

"I'm just a little scared," I said softly.

"I am too," my mother replied, looking at me. "I am too."

As we got to the clinic, Audrey was already there waiting for us. We entered into the waiting room and checked my mother in.

After about a fifteen-minute wait, it was finally Mother's turn to see Dr. Adams. We followed the nurse into the examination room, and soon thereafter, Dr. Adams walked in.

Dr. Adams has been our family doctor ever since I can remember. I used to be afraid of him as a young child, especially every time I needed to get a shot. He was going over my mom's charts, scribbling some notes with a pencil.

"How are you doing, Hazel?" he asked my mom.

"I've been better," my mom said to Dr. Adams as she said to me in the car.

"Your tests have been looking good," he went on the say. "It looks as though the medicine we've prescribed you seems to be working. But just because you start to feel better, young lady, I don't want you think that you can start dancing again."

"You are so funny," my mom said, giving Dr. Adams a perturbed look.

This was my chance, I thought. "Dr. Adams, when would my mom be well enough to travel?"

I explained to Dr. Adams about the situation with my mother and Audrey and how Kyle's family had invited us to stay with them. There, she would always have someone with her.

"Your mom could travel safely in about a week or two," Dr. Adams said kindly. "We just need to run a few more tests to make sure that she is recovering as planned. Where will you be moving to?"

I told Dr. Adams where Kyle lived, and when I did so, his eyes got big.

"I have a colleague there," Dr. Adams said excitedly. "One of the best in the business. At least we know that she'll be in good hands there."

Hearing this news was as though a huge weight had been lifted off my shoulders and Audrey's too. I couldn't wait to tell Kyle the good news.

"Come back next week, and we'll run a few more tests," Dr. Adams said. "You girls want a lollipop?"

I just laughed, but Audrey took one. Now it's time to tell Kyle.

The Good News

As we got back to the house, all I could think about was calling Kyle. I almost forgot my mother in the car.

"Hey, Mom, are you going to be okay? I'm going to call Kyle."

"I'll be in my room," she said, waving her arm at me.

I sat down in the kitchen and dialed Kyle's number. I was so excited to tell him the good news. Finally, we would all be together like one big happy family. Well, at least I hoped so. In reality, you never know how these things will turn out. This is a big step for my mom leaving her home for most of her life.

"Hello," said a kind, gentle voice.

"Hey, Kyle," I said happily. "I have some very good news for you."

"Really? What is it?"

"We should be able to travel in a week or two according to the doctor. All that my mother has to do is pass a few more tests."

"That's awesome news," Kyle said excitedly. "Finally, we will all be together."

Hearing Kyle so excited gave me goose bumps. I couldn't wait to feel him in my arms, to feel his touch.

We continued to talk for a few more minutes when Mother called me to her room.

"Mom's calling me, Kyle," I said sadly. "I think I better go."

"Go to her," Kyle said. "Just remember that I'll be here waiting for you."

As I got off the phone with Kyle, I headed over to Mother's room. To my surprise, she was sitting up in her bed.

"What is it, Mom?" I asked, wondering if something was wrong.

"Sit down, Sandy. I have something to say to you."

I sat down at the foot of her bed.

"What is it, Mother?" I asked.

"I just wanted to tell you how much I appreciate all that you have done for me, Sandy. I know how hard it must be for you being away from Kyle for such a long time."

"Don't worry about me, Mother," I said, trying to fight back tears. "Kyle and I are both in this together. Right now, all that matters is getting you better."

My mother just looked at me and smiled. It wasn't her normal smile. It was more of a tired smile, but it made me feel good anyway. Then she lay down and went to sleep.

"Sleep well, Mother," I said, turning off the light and leaving the room.

Something Is Terribly Wrong

I got up nice and early the next morning. I don't know why, I just did. I went to Mother's room to check on her, and she was still asleep. I decided to take a walk around the neighborhood. I would be leaving this place I called home very soon, and I wanted to take one last stroll around my old stomping grounds.

I walked down to the corner store and bought myself a doughnut and a cup of coffee. For years, I've been coming to this store, and every time I go in there, Mr. Charles, the owner, would ask me when I was going to come and work for him.

I am really going to miss this place, I thought. If I feel this way, I wondered how Mother must feel. I started to feel a little depressed about my mother leaving the place she called home.

I went into the house and went to check on Mom. She was still asleep. *That's strange*, I thought, *Mom was always an early bird even on days when she didn't work.*

"Hey, Mom, are you going to get up?" I said, nudging her shoulder.

There was no response.

"Hey, Mom," I said a little louder. "You want some breakfast?"

Still, there was no response.

I put my hand on her forehead. She felt cold. I tried to feel for her pulse, but it was very faint.

"Mother!" I screamed. "Get up, Mom!"

I ran into the kitchen and dialed 911. Tears were running down my face as the phone rang.

"911 emergency response," said the voice on the other end.

"Please hurry," I said frantically. "There's something wrong with my mother. She's in bed and unresponsive. Please come quickly!"

"Paramedics are on the way, miss. Please stay calm. Do you want me to stay on the line with you?"

"No," I said frantically. "Just hurry."

Minutes seemed like hours, and the ambulance finally arrived. I quickly led them into the room where Mother was sleeping. I tried to keep my composure, but it was no use.

In no time, they had Mom on the stretcher and loaded her onto the ambulance. One of the paramedics came over to me.

"Your mom had another stroke. She's in a coma."

The words just seemed to bounce off my numb body.

"We are going to transport her to city hospital. You can meet us there. We are going to do all we can for your mother."

They quickly drove off, but I just sat there. What had just happened? Why did I leave her alone? What have I done?

I grabbed the phone and called Audrey.

"Hello," she said calmly.

"Audrey," I said, sobbing, "Mom had another stroke. She's being transported to the hospital."

"Oh my god," Audrey said hysterically. "I'll meet you there."

I grabbed the car keys and went to the car. As I sat in the driver's seat, all I could think was, in some way, this was all my fault. I killed my own mother.

Falling Apart

Sitting in the waiting room with Audrey was the hardest thing I've ever had to do. It was as though the world had forgotten about us. All I wanted was to know how Mother was doing. Was she okay? Could we see her? Why was no one telling us anything?

Then out of nowhere, my phone began to ring. It was Kyle.

"Hello," I said, trying not to lose it.

"Hey, Sandy," Kyle said happily, "I haven't heard from you in a while, and I decided to call."

I sat there silently. I didn't know what to say to Kyle. I didn't know what to tell him.

"Hello?" Kyle said, wondering if I was still there.

"Hi," I said quietly.

"Is there something wrong, Sandy?"

I got up and walked to the other side of the room, away from Audrey.

"Mom had another stroke this morning. Right now, we are at the hospital waiting. I don't know how she is doing."

It was Kyle's turn to be silent.

"Oh, Sandy," Kyle said softly. "I'm so sorry."

"Don't be sorry," I told Kyle. "It's not your fault."

I told Kyle about my walk and how I thought that mother was fine when I left. I told him that when I returned, mother was nonresponsive.

"Kyle, it is all my fault. If I didn't go on that walk, maybe Mom would be fine."

"What?" Kyle said sharply. "It is not your fault. There was nothing you could've done."

"You're wrong, Kyle. It is all my fault. I should never had made her move. I shouldn't have been so selfish. I should have put her needs before my own."

"Stop it," Kyle said angrily. "Don't do this to yourself."

It was the first time that I ever heard Kyle raise his voice at me. I don't know why, but it made me angry.

"You know, Kyle, maybe we shouldn't have rushed my mother into moving. Maybe she didn't want to move. Maybe it was too much for her."

"Sandy, your mother wanted what was best for you. I don't think that you made her do anything against her will."

"I need to go, Kyle. I think that the nurse wants to speak to us."

Of course, I lied; there was no nurse, but right now, I didn't really feel like talking to anyone. My world was falling apart and, with it, possibly my hopes and dreams.

Dreaded News

Another hour passed in the waiting room, and still, no one had any answers for us. I went up to the receptionist down the hall and asked her if I could find out anything about my mother.

She could tell that I was very upset, and she asked me to wait while she went into the back to get some answers.

Audrey came up to the desk and said, "Did you find out anything?"

I just nodded and said, "Not yet."

Then the receptionist reappeared from the back.

"The doctor will be out shortly," she said in a comforting tone. "We are swamped back there, but I told him to come out and talk to you."

We both thanked the nurse and went back to our seats. Before we could even sit down, the doctor approached us in the waiting room.

"Hi," he said politely, "I am Dr. Scott. I wish I could speak with you under better circumstances, but it has been a crazy day here at the emergency room."

"How's our mother?" we both asked almost in unison.

"Your mother is brain-dead. I'm sorry, but there is no nice way to put it. She is on life support right now, but I don't really see her coming back from this at all."

Those words hit me like a ton of bricks. Even though we knew that this could happen, we never thought that it actually would. I looked at Audrey, who was already in tears.

"The two of you will have a choice to make," he continued to say. "Do you want her to remain on life support? Or do you want to have it removed?"

I looked up at the doctor, and then I looked at Audrey, who was still sobbing.

"Can we let you know?" I said softly.

"Of course," he said kindly. "These decisions are never easy. Think about it, talk it over with your family, and then let me know."

We both thanked Dr. Scott for coming out to talk to us. I wondered how often he must come out here with bad news for family members waiting for their loved ones. *It must be a terrible job to do*, I thought.

"Doctor, can we at least see her?" Audrey said, somewhat regaining her composure.

"Sure you can," Dr. Scott said, managing a smile. "Follow me."

We followed Dr. Scott into the emergency room, where he led us to Mother's room. There were tubes and wires everywhere, but at the same time, she looked so peaceful.

"Now if you excuse me," Dr. Scott said kindly, "I need to check up on some other patients."

We both just sat there at Mother's side, hoping that somehow she would just wake up, and things would be back to normal. But we both knew that it wasn't going to happen.

"What do you think?" I asked Audrey.

"I don't know," Audrey said sadly. "Let's not think about it right now."

Audrey was right. Sadly, these were going to be the final days that we get to spend with our mom.

Waiting

I haven't heard back from Sandy since I spoke to her earlier this morning. Everyone keeps asking me how Sandy's mother is, but I have nothing to tell them.

I have a hard enough time doing inventory on a normal day, but with Sandy and her mom on my mind, it is almost impossible.

"Why don't you go home, son?" my father said calmly. "We can lock up the store tonight."

"Thanks, Dad," I said, trying not to let him see the messy inventory list.

I went into the office and put away my things. I checked my phone again but no new messages or voice mails.

As I drove home, I began to think about what Sandy had told me earlier in the day. Why did she blame herself for all of this? The more I thought about it, the more I came to one conclusion. I really didn't know Sandy all that well. Everything happened so fast; it was like we skipped the getting-to-know-you process and fast-forwarded to marriage.

For the first time, I questioned whether Sandy was actually my true love. Talk about a reality check at the worst possible time.

As I arrived home, Mom was waiting anxiously for me.

"Any news yet?" she asked.

"None," I replied.

"Are you going to call her?"

"Yes, Mom, I am going to call her, and when I find out something, you will be the first to know."

I headed upstairs and into my room. As I sat on my bed, I took out my phone and stared at it. For some reason, I was hesitant to call her. Maybe Sandy needed space. I just lay there and quickly fell asleep.

I quickly jumped at the sound of my phone ringing. I rubbed my eyes to see who was calling. Dang, telemarketer.

I went back downstairs where dinner was almost ready. Dad was sitting at the table, reading the paper.

"Nothing yet?" he said from behind the front page.

"Nothing," I said, taking a biscuit.

Kevin came running into the house; his friend dropped him off from baseball practice.

"Wash up, young man," my mother said, pointing her finger at him.

We had a nice, peaceful dinner. The topic of Sandy didn't come up once, and I appreciated my parents for that. I decided to go back upstairs, do some reading, and go to bed. Inventory was kicking my butt, and I wasn't about to let it beat me.

The Bad News

I went to the store early today. I wanted to get a head start on inventory and try to get into a groove. One small problem though. My mind only seemed to wander toward Sandy. Why hasn't she called me yet? Am I supposed to call her?

I forced myself to move on, first paints and then paintbrushes. Nothing was going to stop me. I was going to kick inventory's ass, and then it happened, the call I had been waiting for. I threw my papers on the ground and fumbled to answer my phone.

"Um, hello?" I said in my geekiest tone.

"Hello," said a kind, sweet voice. "Sorry I didn't call you sooner. A lot has been happening here, and when you hear what I have to say, I'm sure that you'll understand."

"It's okay," I said reassuringly. "How is your mom?"

There was a slight pause. And for some reason, I knew that something was wrong.

"Audrey and I have decided to take mother off of life support today. It is what she wanted."

"Oh, Sandy, I'm so sorry. I wish I could be there for you."

"We have a lot to do, Kyle. There are forms to fill out, papers to sign. I wouldn't be much fun."

"I miss you, Sandy."

There was another slight pause.

"Kyle," Sandy said sadly, "don't make this any harder for me."

"What do you mean, Sandy?" I asked.

"I've been thinking a lot about everything that has happened within the past few months, about you and me, about Mom. Everything happened so fast between us, Kyle, don't you agree?"

"I do, Sandy, but everything seemed so right."

"But everything is not right," Sandy said, her voice breaking down. "At least not with me. Kyle, please don't hate me, but right now, I think it's best if we take a break from each other. Kyle, I don't know who I am anymore. I need to find myself, regain my life."

"I can help you, Sandy?" I said frantically.

"No, Kyle. It is something that I need to do myself. Kyle, no matter what happens, I will always love you. But please, let me go."

I couldn't believe what Sandy was asking me to do. After all we've been through, she was going to throw it all away.

"I will send you back your ring, Kyle. Please let me do this. I need to do this."

Now it was my turn to be silent. I was not prepared for any of this. I had anger, sadness, and frustration coursing through my veins.

"Kyle, are you there?" Sandy said softly.

"Sandy," I said, trying not to lose it, "I will do what you ask. And the only reason I am doing this is because I love you so much. Take whatever time you need. All that I ask is when you find yourself, please let me know."

"Thank you, Kyle. Goodbye."

Just like that, she was gone.

I called my dad and told him the bad news. He gave me a hug and told me to go home. When I got home, Mom already knew. She also gave me a hug.

As I went up into my room, I closed my door, threw myself onto the bed, and cried. Never before had I felt as sad as I did today. I didn't know what to do or who to turn to. I just lay there helpless, sobbing like a little boy who lost his best friend. I lost more than my best friend today. I lost my true love.

Printed in the United States
By Bookmasters